The Reluctant Bride

*To my darling grand-daughter,
Love Grandma Maxine Douglas*

MAXINE DOUGLAS

The Reluctant Bride
by Maxine Douglas

Copyright 2016 © D.H. Fritter
All Rights Reserved
Cover Design by Maria Connor
Edited by Ally Robertson
Published by D.H. Fritter
Formatting by D.H. Fritter

All rights reserved. No part of this book may be reproduced or transmitted in any form or by any means, electronic or mechanical, including photocopying, recording, or by any information storage and retrieval system, without permission in writing from the copyright owner or publisher. The characters and events portrayed in this book are fictitious. Any similarity to real persons, living or dead, or events, is coincidental and not intended by the author.

The scanning, uploading or distribution of this book via the internet, or via any other means without the permission of the copyright owner and publisher is illegal and punishable by law. Please purchase only authorized electronic editions, and do no participate in or encourage electronic piracy of copyrighted materials. Your support of the author's rights is appreciated.

Second Edition June 2017
First Edition September 2016
ISBN-10: 1537707566
ISBN-13: 978-1537707563

DEDICATION

To my husband, who will always be my hero and the love of my life.

And to all the cowboy I grew up watching in the 1950s and 1960s, who were my heroes:
Zorro, The Virginian, Adam Cartwright.
I've never forgotten you and never will.

ACKNOWLEDGMENTS

A heartfelt thank you and big hugs and kisses to Callie Hutton and Heidi Vanlandingham for asking me to be part of an amazing boxset, and for encouraging me to jump head first into a genre I was totally unfamiliar writing. I can't wait to do another project with you both.

Huge hugs to my beta reader, Julie Castle, for making sure everything made sense and flowed. I'm forever grateful for your time, insight, and friendship.

To the following establishments for allowing me to sit for hours writing *The Reluctant Bride*: the staff of McDonalds of Chickasha, who greeted me each morning with my dose of caffeine, and to the librarians of the Chickasha Public Library, who were always gracious in helping me find the research material I asked for.

PROLOGUE

Southcentral Wisconsin
Late April, 1877

"Have you lost your senses?" Miss Roseanne Duncan looked over the advertisement for a mail order bride, the paper rattling in her hand. "I can't become a mail order bride. Besides, he's expecting you."

"Doesn't matter," Abigail Johnson replied, continuing to sort through the tub of fresh vegetables. "This is your best chance to survive and you know it."

A sick feeling went through her at Abby's blunt words, memories of the mistress falling to her death, the master at the top of the stairs assailed her. She shuddered. The memorial was set for today. It was only a matter of time until… No she couldn't think it. A chance to get away…could she really take it? Rose read over the advertisement flier again. "Abby, this looks more like a wanted poster than a man in search of a wife."

"Granted, it shows he is a bit creative, and educated by the way it's worded." Abigail peeked over the top of the page, then returned to picking out the best of the potatoes.

Rose was still stunned by Abby's plan to become a mail order bride. "Yes, I'll give him that much at least he's literate. Why would you feel the need to answer something like this in the first place?" Rose had heard dubious stories of mail order brides and very few of them ended well. "You're a wonderful cook and passionate woman, any local man would be lucky to have you. You don't need to answer an advertisement from a Wild West gentleman, if he is one, that you don't know and move off to who knows where."

"Maybe I wanted to grab my last chance for adventure," she said with a grin.

Rose felt bad not wanting to hurt her feelings. "Oh, I didn't mean to…"

"Don't you worry about it. I'll take the next one who suits my fancy. This is exactly what you need after what happened. Rose, what have you got to lose?" Abigail whispered, scrubbing the dirt from the potatoes for supper that night. "You need to leave this house as soon as you can. They'll be burying the lady in a few days, but people are already talking. It's no secret she'd become ill, Rose. But sickness didn't break her neck and everybody's talking about it. Even Mrs. Griswold's family has grown suspicious."

"I've heard the rumors, but we both know the truth. Mrs. Griswold wasn't ill enough to fall to the bottom of the staircase on her own Abby. I know what I saw."

THE RELUCTANT BRIDE
(Brides Along the Chisholm Trail)

Rose grabbed her friend's hand and squeezed it lightly. "He knows I saw him do it."

"All the more reason to get out of town before someone questions you." Abigail ceased her scrubbing, her brow furrowed she looked Rose square in the face. "Have you considered the consequences of that testimony if her family presses forward with an investigation? You know he could make it look like you're the one who 'helped' his wife down the stairs that night. He'll make them believe you were in love with him, throwing yourself at him at every opportunity to lure him from his poor sickly wife."

Rose recoiled from the thought of that snide monster touching her. "No one will believe that story. They can't, it's not true." Even as she said it she knew it wasn't true. She was a mere servant and an impoverished one at that. He was wealthy. No one would believe her if it came to her word against his. It was why she hadn't gone to the law even though it pricked her conscience to keep silent. It just plain went against her personal code of justice to let him go unpunished. The horrific scene played across her mind again.

Rose had been starting her morning duties when she heard them arguing at the top of the stairs. Mrs. Griswold didn't want to go down for an early breakfast that day; she wanted to go back to her room. Mr. Griswold kept insisting she make an appearance so the staff wouldn't think she was sickly. Rose had often wondered if the source of the wasting sickness had come from the master's own hand. All he'd have to do was slip something into her tea. She shuddered knowing it was too late to save her mistress now.

That morning, they'd continued to argue and then came the scream. The horrible sound of a body tumbling down the stairs, and Mr. Griswold standing at the top of the landing with smug indifference on his face. When he turned and saw her, the look in his eyes when they locked on hers was dark, dead and cold as a winter's frigid night, promising retribution if she said anything. She'd shivered and dashed back up the servant's staircase, hiding in her room until the other maids began to move about the house. Then a scream rang out from the scullery maid and Rose knew the mistress had been found.

So far there hadn't been any question as to how Mrs. Griswold came to be at the bottom of the staircase. Mr. Griswold told the doctor and police officers that she'd tripped over a rug at the top of the landing. She hadn't had a lantern with her so she could see in the hallway. And since Mr. Griswold was a wealthy man, his explanation had gone unchallenged. Even so, Mrs. Griswold's family threatened to hire an investigator for all the good that would do Mrs. Griswold now.

Rose chased the fresh memory from her mind and looked over the advertisement again. Abby was right, she had no other choice but to run. But this, could she even contemplate being a mail order bride, tying herself to a man she didn't even know? According to the paper, a man named Logan Granger was looking for a mail order bride to help manage his household and his six-year-old daughter. It indicated he was a widower of means, healthy, and respected at the age of thirty. Mr.

Granger wrote that he lived in a stylish house in the frontier town of Dodge City, Kansas. Far from Mr. Griswold's reach she thought taking heart. There was no mention of wifely duties, just the household and the child. Mr. Logan Granger basically wanted a housekeeper and nanny for the price of marriage and a home.

But, Kansas? Could she move so far away just to escape the fury of Atticus Griswold, who would certainly become her former employer before long and probable accuser? How could she be sure she wasn't walking into something far worse than she'd be leaving? *What could be worse than the gallows,* she thought wryly as her conscience smote her. Marrying someone she didn't love. So who needed love?

Looking at the ad it seemed love wasn't one of the requirements. Besides when she got there if they didn't suit she could cry off. She was afraid her heart wouldn't allow her to marry a man she didn't at least feel affection for. Could she make an exception for one who made no mention of love? And then there was Dodge City itself. She'd read the papers. Dodge City had a reputation for being a wild town brimming with gamblers, gunfighters, and saloon girls of the night.

"Abby, even if it were possible there's no reason for this man to even want me. I'm a housemaid with no experience at taking care of a little girl. Not to mention, he sounds like he's a pretty important man in his town. What would he want with a housemaid for a bride who doesn't even know how to cook?" Rose placed the paper on the counter top, her heart heavy with sadness. She had no right to think a man like the one Mr. Granger sounded like would actually want a servant for a wife. Then again, maybe that's exactly all he wanted. After all, he did indicate he was looking for someone to manage his household and look after his little girl, nothing more. Would that mean she'd have her own bedroom, or would she have to share a room with Mr. Granger, her prospective husband?

"You can follow a recipe, can't you?" Abigail shot her a side glance, the corner of her mouth moving into a small smile. "What if he didn't care what you did for a living?"

"And how would you know that? This man doesn't want a runaway witness for a bride. He'll want someone to match his stature. Someone substantial who comes with the full knowledge of how a household runs." Rose took the paper between her fingers, giving it one last look over before tossing it into the day's waste.

"And you don't have that knowledge?" Abigail wiped her hands on her apron, then reached into her pocket. "I don't know, but there's only one way to find out." She offered Rose an envelope with Abigail's name and address scrolled across it. "He wants me and I'm only a cook and much older than he is. So obviously he isn't fussy. Why wouldn't he want a pretty young wife instead of a matronly one?"

"Abby, what have you done?" Rose took the envelope, pulling out a piece of parchment folded neatly into thirds. Tucked into the folds of the letter was a ticket for the next train to Kansas City, where she'd then switch trains and continue to travel the rest of the way to

Dodge City.

"Giving my dear friend the chance to live, if she'll take it."

CHAPTER ONE

Dodge City, Kansas
Early May, 1877

Logan Granger tugged at his vest once again. What a fool hair-brained idea it was to advertise for a bride and expect her to come to Dodge City of all places, but he was between a rock and a hard place. If not for Lilly, he wouldn't have done it. But Dodge was no place for a six-year-old girl to be running around without supervision. He couldn't watch her and do his job without having to worry where she was all the time. It wasn't fair to keep her locked in a room at the Lady Gay either. She needed room to run and play, and grow into a fine young woman like her momma.

Logan pulled the watch from the vest pocket. His father had given him the keepsake the day Logan had graduated from Harvard law school. He smiled remembering that day. Pop had been so proud of him.

THE RELUCTANT BRIDE
(Brides Along the Chisholm Trail)

All Logan had to do was find a respectable law firm to establish himself in, then find a girl from a good family to marry and settle down. He'd done it all; he'd taken up with the law firm of Winston & Blodgett in Chicago in 1870, after he married Katie Blanchard of Boston, became a father to Lilly the following year, and then lost Katie to scarlet fever somewhere within five years of their marriage—the exact date escaped him. He wanted to find a way to escape the pain of losing her, and soon realized what he'd really been looking for was a way to join her.

So he resigned from the firm and went to work undercover for the Pinkerton Detective Agency in Chicago. He'd worked with the detective agency through the law firm for a few years on various court cases he'd taken on. Many of his cases had him working especially hand-in-hand with Mr. Pinkerton himself, and Logan found a real camaraderie with the man every outlaw feared. His work gave him a new found purpose and he soon realized Lilly needed her daddy more than Logan needed to join Katie. It was only then that he realized the error of his ways. He might need the oblivion of danger to make himself feel whole again but Lilly's needs had to come first. Pushing the sadness aside, Logan flipped the gold inscribed cover closed and pushed the watch back into his waistcoat.

"Sure hope you know what you're doing bringing that woman here, Logan." Marshal Dane Jones stood next to Logan, rocking back on his heels. The marshal had recently sent four women on the last wagon train from the fort to Santa Fe. Chaperoned by Nellie Ward,

Jones felt it was in the young women's best interests to find husbands to look after them. Logan smiled, he'd heard the Widow Markham had married before she even left town.

"So do I, Marshal. After all, I got the notion from you." Logan looked up and down the tracks avoiding making eye contact with the marshal. "I didn't see any other way. Lilly's gonna be a young lady before I know it, and she needs a mature woman to guide her along the right path."

"I know a few ladies in town more than willing to be your wife, you didn't need to send for a store bought one." Jones chuckled, slapping Logan on the back.

Logan looked at the marshal shaking his head. "I'm particular, Marshal. I don't need that kind of distraction in my line of work."

"How particular can it be to find a wife? As long as she's willing to lay with you, cook your meals, and wash your clothes what is she there for?" The marshal winked, then chuckled again.

"You never cease to astound me, Marshal. How about a little something called companionship, trust, honor? Bed doesn't come into the equation." No, he couldn't even contemplate letting a woman get that close to his heart again. To make sure of it, he'd hand picked the right candidate. "I've got a little girl to think of. Taking this wife to bed is not what I'm looking for." Logan shuffled his feet, then took his hat off slapping the dust off the brim before settling it back over his thick black hair. "Abigail Johnson will be my wife in name only. She's older, respectable, and well versed in the running of a household, and she'll be the perfect woman to properly guide Lilly along."

"I can see where Lilly would be of a concern to you, Logan. Are you sure this woman won't run off with the first slick gambler she meets? I've got enough trouble in this town without you bringing this city woman in to add to it."

"Of that I'm sure, Dane. Miss Johnson will be the perfect 'mature' woman to take care of Lilly should anything happen to me."

"I see." Marshall Jones tucked his thumbs into his gun belt, then turned looking Logan in the face. "Any leads on that cattle rustling business yet?"

"Nothing solid, or worth mentioning." Logan dragged his gaze across the street, watching the upstanding citizens of Dodge come and go from the stores lining Front Street. Dodge City was starting to grow into a true metropolis of more than drovers and gamblers. Families were settling just outside of town farming the land and raising dairy cows. There were more women and children walking the streets every day. The train did its share to bring them from Boston to the wild west. It amazed him that more stayed then left when things got a bit tough on them. It took true grit to make a home in the untamed west.

"Well, I'll leave you to it. Preacher Samuels sent me over to let you know he'll be in the Long Branch awaitin'. Shouldn't be too long now." Marshal Jones turned, leaving Logan to mull over his upcoming nuptials.

Any moment now his bride would be arriving.

She'd step off the Santa Fe, walk across the street and straight into the Long Branch to get married. No courtship. No getting to know each other. No time to fall in love. It was better that way.

According to the letter from Abigail Johnson of Wisconsin, she was of an age past the time of bearing a child, and that suited Logan just fine. She implied she'd always longed for a daughter to love and guide through her young years. Miss Johnson also indicated she managed the kitchen of a rather large estate for several years, but wanted to seek out on an adventure before she walked into her later years. In short she sounded perfect.

Miss Johnson hadn't sent a photograph, stating it didn't matter what either of them looked like since this was to be a marriage of convenience and in name only, which suited him just fine. She was willing to share his name, help raise Lilly, make his meals, and any other household duties, but she refused to share his bed. She'd wrote if that was accommodating to him, she gladly accepted his terms and proposal of marriage.

Logan was definitely accommodating to those terms; he'd set them after all. He'd had the extra room next to Lilly's prepared for his "wife" and at the opposite end of the hall from him. That way they'd barely have to cross paths in the bedroom area if they didn't want to. He aimed to have his daughter safely under the protection and guidance, if not love, of Miss Johnson should something happen to him during his cattle rustling investigation.

When he'd accepted the undercover assignment to Dodge City, he'd not thought of Lilly's future nor what

THE RELUCTANT BRIDE
(Brides Along the Chisholm Trail)

would happen to his young daughter if he were killed. That had been six months ago. It didn't take him long to realize that Dodge wasn't the place for motherless children, even though several families had settled in the area, and he couldn't bear to send her to the family ranch in northern Montana. Dodge was still the stomping ground of every cowpoke, gambler and gunfighter passing through town.

It had taken some time, but once Logan had secured his place as barkeep at the Lady Gay, he'd saved enough money to add to his Chicago bank accounts; he got Lilly and him out of the Dodge House and into a home of their own. The sparsely furnished, two-story sat on the north edge of town, but lacked a woman's touch. His new wife would soon set that right. He missed the smell of a home cooked meal coming from the kitchen and sitting down to eat like a family without half the town for company. He felt certain Miss Johnson would provide that for Lilly.

The train whistle blared as it roared into town, chasing away Logan's thoughts of the warm and welcoming home he admitted to be missing.

Logan adjusted his hat and tie. "Looks like my bride has arrived right on time."

ROSE DUNCAN CLENCHED the letter tightly in her hand. Going over in her mind the past few days of how her life was in a flux of change, she gazed up at the train she was about to finish her escape in. She was still in disbelief that she'd taken Abby up on her outrageous suggestion. Part of her felt freer than she had in…well forever. She could do this. Manage this man's household and daughter. She loved children and they usually took to her. She felt bad that she'd done Abby out of this adventure, but Abby assured her she'd find a more suitable, older man to marry as there seemed to be plenty of them available out west.

After a brief stop in Kansas City where she switched trains, Rose glanced over her shoulder then stepped up into a train for the last time, making a wish for luck. Whatever came, she knew she'd never see Wisconsin again. She'd left everything behind in her small room on the third floor of her former employer's house. In haste, she had put on the only clean dress and undergarments she had before taking the stage to Chicago for what felt like months ago. Abigail insisted she travel without bags so as not to cause suspicion as she left the big house. She also insisted Rose not worry about not having any clothes with her, for surely Mr. Granger would take care of her need of a clean dress and undergarments.

Rose desperately wanted to scrub the sooty traveling grime off her body, and from her mind, the haunting picture of her employer pushing his wife down the stairs that troubled her every time she closed her eyes. She wanted a fresh bath, her hair smelling like lavender instead of smoke, and a clean dress to wear instead of one speckled with dust and soot. Surely those requests wouldn't be too much to ask for. Certainly she'd be able to get all those things before she stepped in front of a preacher and married a man she didn't know.

Rose shuddered, glad to have left that big house of

death, and the person who caused it. She found herself continuously looking around at other travelers as she journeyed from Wisconsin, then through the Kansas country side. Even now hundreds of miles away she waited for a law man to arrest her, drag her back to testify against a man she now feared. She scoured every face for any indication they were looking for her.

"Next stop, Topeka, Kansas. Passengers going to Dodge City please stay aboard the train, we will only be here long enough to embark and disembark, and take on water."

The train pulled into Topeka, steam from the engine hissing in the air. Rose gazed out the window as the train chugged into town. She tucked her skirts around her, making a protective barrier against anyone who would sit beside her. She'd be glad to finally be rid of the dirt and noise of the wheels churning over the iron rails. To be able to feel the ground solid and unmoving beneath her feet for longer than it took her to use the bathroom to quickly tidy up, a hot bath a simple pleasure she now craved.

A man sporting a star on his lapel sat down across from her. "Ma'am," he tipped his hat and smiled. His eyes were crystal blue. A mustache fell over his upper lip to the corners of his mouth. Rose quickly looked away, her heart pounding. What if he was after her? What if Mr. Griswold forced Abby to tell him where Rose had gone, and he'd hired this man to track her down? Friendly as he may seem, she was afraid that his intense staring would invoke further conversation. She continued to look out the window as the train pulled out of the station. She wanted no conversation with this man, none at all.

"Shouldn't you be getting off here, ma'am?" the man inquired, his easy way of speaking floated over her.

Rose cast him a look, then turned away. She hated being rude to the man. If he wasn't an officer of the law she'd have been happy for a bit of conversation with someone other than herself.

"I don't mean to intrude, but the next stop is Dodge City and I can't suppose a fine young woman like yourself would be traveling there on purpose." The lawman continued to scrutinize her.

Rose sighed, her heart pounding slower in her breast as her fear abated. He didn't know who she was, he wasn't out to drag her back home. It was only too obvious he was not going to give up the gift of gab any time soon.

"Excuse my rudeness, ma'am. My name is Hawkins, Gabe Hawkins. I'm a deputy marshal in Dodge." Deputy Marshal Gabe Hawkins tipped his hat once more, his smile wide and friendly.

"As it happens, I am traveling to Dodge City. I'm meeting my new husband there." Rose chirped, driving home the point that she was already spoken for and not interested in his company.

Hawkins slapped his knee, then laughed. "Well, I'll be dogged! Which one of those Texas cowpokes has decided to take up with a wife all legal like?"

"I don't believe Mr. Granger is a cowpoke." She retorted, disgusted by the fact this man of law thought she looked like she'd marry a dirty cattle runner. "I'll have you know he's a well-respected man in Dodge City."

Deep rolling laughter filled the car. Rose scowled at the deputy, fighting the urge to slap him for his impetuousness. What in the blazes was so funny? Unless, Mr. Granger had lied in his letter...no, that couldn't be. But then she wasn't telling the truth herself.

"Well, that he is ma'am. Well respected by many a man, and woman, in Dodge."

She relaxed at his words. "Good. Now if you'd be so kind as to leave me to my own thoughts, I'd deeply appreciate it." Rose gave him her best sweet smile, then took Mr. Granger's letter yet again from her tattered pocketbook. Unfolding it for the hundredth time, she reread the words her soon-to-be husband wrote to another woman:

My Dear Miss Johnson,

Thank you for your letter inquiring my advertisement for a bride. As you know, I am in need of a mature woman who knows and understands the running of a household, as well as the needs of a six-year-old girl. That is all I require of you. Rest assured I do not expect you to come all the way from Wisconsin without the promise and protection of marriage.

By your letter, you appear to be perfectly suitable for my situation. I have provided you with the necessary transportation documents. I hope you have not changed your mind, and I look forward to our joyous occasion upon your arrival.

Respectfully yours,
Logan Granger

Rose fingered the tintype photograph of the man she'd never seen before, but would call husband in a few short hours. His boyish grin only accented the dimples playing on his cheeks. His eyes glittered with a hint of sorrow in their depths. He appeared to have a good head of hair, clean shaven, and well-groomed for a man living in a frontier town. Unless his dress was a lie, Mr. Granger had a sense of fashion.

Nervously she folded the letter with the photograph tucked back safely in its folds. She was a bride on the run. A mail order bride Logan Granger was not expecting at the station.

LOGAN STOOD ON the depot platform as the Santa Fe finally came to a steamy halt. Smoke from the screeching of steel against steel burst around him.

"Well ole boy, the time has come. I hope you're ready to take on an older sister-type for a wife," Logan said to himself under his breath thankful he was the only one waiting for someone to arrive. It was no secret he was expecting a lady on today's train, he didn't want an audience mulling around that may scare her off. Lilly needed this woman too much. While the future Mrs. Granger may not be physically appealing, he did find himself hopeful she wouldn't have a goiter or warts so he'd be able to look at her and say the words without wincing.

Marshal Jones had come to say his piece. Preacher Samuels was preparing the words he'd recite to the bride and groom over a glass of beer at the Long Branch. Not to mention he had Montana Sue looking after Lilly down at the Lady Gay until he got his new wife to take his name.

Logan sucked in his breath along with his courage. He'd faced down armed men he could do this. The conductor stepped down from one of the passenger cars, followed by an array of men and women from all walks of life. A few looked like city slickers, not unlike he was six months ago, looking for adventure and opportunity. He watched as each person passed by him, and made their way across the street to the hotel. When he looked up again, the prettiest blonde-haired young lady in a plain looking calico dress cautiously stepped down, her skirts gathered in her hand above the dusty street.

Her long hair pulled back in a simple ponytail, pieces of unruly strands fell around her face. She nervously glanced around the platform like a rabbit being cautious of a trap laid out for her. There was a quiet beauty about her that seemed simple and real. What was a young lady like her thinking coming to Dodge City without an escort?

Coming up behind her was Deputy Marshal Gabe Hawkins. Logan's beating heart slowed when Gabe said a few words to the woman, smiled, then made his way over to Logan. Of course, Gabe would pick up a beauty on his travels, it was the way the cards were always laid out for the deputy.

"Logan!" Gabe greeted, his hand extended in friendship. "Good to see a friendly face waiting for me."

"Deputy, looks like you brought a little lady back with you." Logan remarked, surprised at the wave of envy flushing through him. Leave it to Lady Luck, Gabe would get the good looking girl while Logan waited for his matronly wife-to-be. No time for self-pity, it's what he wanted and embraced when he'd accepted Abigail Johnson's response to his advertisement.

Deputy Hawkins smiled, then burst out laughing. Slapping Logan on the back, he said as he walked away, "She's not with me, Granger. She's here to meet her new husband. Someone named Logan Granger."

Logan swallowed the rock in his throat. His hands were moist and he felt a ping in his britches he'd forgotten existed. His pretty little wife-to-be approached and all he could do was work the brim of his hat over and over in his hands.

CHAPTER TWO

ROSE GATHERED HER skirts then stepped off the train. There was dirt and dust everywhere she looked. People dodged horses as they tried to maneuver from one side of the street to another. *Where have I come to? How can this be any better than what I left? Because no one here will try to hurt me. I'll be safe under the protection of a husband.*

"Welcome to Dodge City, ma'am." Deputy Hawkins tipped his hat, then strolled over to a man standing on the depot landing. They exchanged a few words, then the deputy slapped the man on the back before proceeding across the street to the jail.

The man he'd been talking with stood staring at her. She shaded her eyes from the sun and her breath hitched in her chest. The man walking toward her, hat in his hand, looked like her husband-to-be. Logan Granger.

"Miss Johnson? Miss Abigail Johnson?" he asked, a worried look on his face.

Rose looked around for a moment, unable to speak.

What have you got to lose, Rose? Abby's words soared through her mind. She smiled, then extended a hand to her soon-to-be husband who, handsome as he was, looked like a scared rabbit at the moment.

Rose sucked in her bottom lip. Logan Granger was much more pleasing to look at than his picture portrayed. Maybe a bit older now, his eyes held the same boyish twinkle in them. The sorrow so close to the surface now appeared to have taken a step back into the shadows. He easily stood a good six inches over her, but in a gentle, loving manner. Rose felt warmth in her inner core that took her by surprise.

"Mr. Logan Granger?" She withdrew her hand when Logan made no attempt to take it. *He's disappointed in me. Probably thinking he's made a big mistake in sending for a bride without first seeing what she at least looked like.*

Rose sighed, tucked away the stray strands of hair falling along her cheek and straightened to her full five foot four-inch frame. Maybe Logan Granger isn't as well educated as they first thought. His manners were certainly lacking.

"You're Miss Abigail Johnson?" His smiling question lit a fire in her stomach. She was in a lot of trouble, and she knew it. Oh not the kind that would land her on the wrong end of a switch. No, it was the kind that could end up breaking her heart.

"Yes, yes I am. I'm sorry if I'm somewhat of a disappointment to you and not what you expected. I thought my letter was quite clear." Rose stood on the platform worrying the clasp of her pocketbook, unsure of what she should do. Butterflies fluttered wildly in her stomach in anticipation. If he sent her away she'd be lost or worse. She had no money. No way to go back to Wisconsin, not sure that she could dare go back, or go any other place for that matter. "I can see that you are taken by surprise. If you'd be so kind as to tell me where I might find a place to inquire about work, you'll be free to find another more suitable wife to manage your household and raise your daughter."

"Huh? No, no, not at all. You've come all this way. It's just that, you did in fact take me by surprise. I pictured more of a matronly lady had answered my advertisement." Logan took her by the elbow, and a shot of electricity clipped through her. "I'm sorry for my poor manners. I am Logan Granger and you will do just fine, Miss Johnson. I'll have someone get your belongings as soon as we see Preacher Samuels."

"Really, that won't be necessary Mr. Granger. These are the only items I brought with me." Rose ran her hands over the skirt of her bedraggled dress. The calico print soiled in spots from the endless days and nights spent aboard the train. With no fresh dress to change into, this was the best she'd look on her wedding day.

"As for my letter, a good friend of mine wrote to you on my behalf." She wasn't exactly lying about it. "She knew I wouldn't, and thought your proposal perfect for my situation."

"Hmm, and what might that situation be, Miss Johnson?" Logan observed her with suspicion. Her face started to burn, she looked away afraid that he'd see the fear that raced through her.

Rose glanced down at her pocketbook, her fingers working the already warn clasp. "I was being replaced in my employer's household. The lady of the house suddenly passed and her husband decided to cut the house staff in half."

"Oh, well then," he said studying her then wiping a smudge of dirt from her face. "We mustn't keep the preacher waiting, he's been there all morning as it is. And please, call me Logan. After all we are soon to be wed." Logan guided her across the street and into a place called the Long Branch.

Rose had never stepped foot in a saloon before, but was well aware of the sinful activities she heard went on in them…drinking, gambling, as well as, saloon girls providing entertainment. She saw none of that as Logan led her through the swinging doors. There were very few customers and not a saloon girl to be seen.

Leaning against the bar was Deputy Hawkins from the train, his smile friendly and his eyes filled with amusement. Beside him another lawman gawked while sipping a frothy mug. The barkeep stopped wiping down the bar and lined up small glasses of beverages. Then there was the man Rose guessed to be the Preacher Samuels, a bible sitting in front of him next to a dark frothy mug of drink.

She fought back lingering remnants of fear, they didn't know her real identity, and Mr. Griswold's reach couldn't extend this far west. *Please let it be so*, she said to herself her eyes closed in silent prayer. When she opened them, they all stared at her like she was some

THE RELUCTANT BRIDE
(Brides Along the Chisholm Trail)

sort of oddity at the fair. Yes, she was a bit dusty from her trip, but she certainly didn't look like she'd not bathed in a month or two. She'd taken a quick sponge bath a time or two along the way, nothing like a good long hot bath though.

"Logan, do you want to give your bride time to freshen up before she promises herself to you?" Preacher Samuels asked after swallowing a glass of dark liquid Rose presumed to be a liquor of some sort.

Rose glanced over at Logan, noticing he fidgeted, a bit uneasy. *You can do this, Rose. He's as hesitant as you are, so you're on equal ground at the moment.* She took a deep breath, closed her eyes for a moment then slipped her hand gently in his and turned to the preacher. "That's not necessary. The sooner we get married the sooner I can get things settled in the house." Rose smiled up at Logan. He appeared to have broken out in a sweat. What did he have to be nervous about? He'd sent for her, hadn't he? "Don't you agree Mr. Granger?"

"Huh? Oh yes. Yes, by all means let's do as the lady says." Logan grinned at her, then gently squeezed Rose's hand. Her heart skipped a beat, fluttering wildly against her breast.

Rose turned back to the preacher, her nerve lodged in her throat she barely listened as the wedding ceremony began.

LOGAN COULDN'T BELIEVE his luck. The beautiful vision standing next to him would soon become his wife. Somewhere someone was playing a cruel joke on him. Abigail Johnson was anything but matronly. Despite her rumpled appearance, she was the most stunning young lady he'd ever seen. And she was about to become his wife. How in the world was he going to be able to hold to his part of the bargain with her living in his home?

The moment he gazed into her coffee colored eyes, he'd lost his heart to her. Thankfully she'd tucked that stray lock of hair, or he'd have embarrassed himself. He'd wanted to reach over to feel the silkiness of it. His mouth ached to taste her. *I am in so much trouble here. All I can think about it touching her...everywhere.*

Before Logan knew what he was doing, Preacher Samuels guided them through the ceremony. They'd said their marriage vows. Pledged themselves to each other. Logan repeated the words to love and protect, to obey, to not lay with another, all the words that he'd intended never to say to another woman. Said "I do" and then he'd kissed his new wife on a soft, pink cheek. Marshal Jones and Deputy Marshal Hawkins witnessed the marriage.

Then came the round of drinks, his new wife—Mrs. Logan Granger—declined even a sarsaparilla. Had he married a stiff, unloving woman? No, he wouldn't believe it. There was too much kindness in her face for him to believe she'd have a harsh word for even the girls at the Lady Gay.

"Logan, I think your new wife could use a good meal after eating on the train," the marshal suggested, looking at him like he was a lost child. In fact, that's exactly how he felt. Lost in the warm depths of Abigail's dark brown eyes.

"Yes, of course. Come Mrs. Granger, let's get

something to eat at the Dodge House." It felt strange to say those words after all these years. The last time, he'd lost his wife before their fifth year of marriage. *Please God, let Abigail live a long life for Lilly.* Warmth spread through his heart. Logan grinned, then took his wife's dainty hand in his larger one. "I'll have Montana Sue bring Lilly up for dinner. Then we'll head out to the house and get you settled in."

Rose peered up at him, tears brimming in the corner of her eyes. If it was one thing that tugged at his heartstrings it was a female about to cry.

He leaned down, tenderly kissing each eye. "It'll be fine, Abigail. You'll see," he whispered, taking her in his arms—the fit perfect.

Taking her hand, he placed it in the crook of his elbow. The feel of her next to him felt anything but wrong. It was right. Beyond perfection. This woman, who by her letter he presumed to be more sister-like rather than young and vibrant, would soon turn his house into a home. Not only for him, but for Lilly. A young wife who would be able to keep up with a very active, and somewhat tomboyish, little girl. A young wife who sparked a fancy out of his dark soul. He'd have a lock put on her bedroom door first thing in the morning, if she desired one.

"Please Mr. Granger, call me—Rose. Rose is my favorite flower and it's my middle name. I'm named after my granny." She strolled next to him as if they were out for a Sunday walk after church. He really was in hot water and he hadn't even done anything wrong or dishonorable—yet.

"Of course, Abby—err, Rose. As long as you call me Logan in return. Unless of course I'm in hot water for something." Logan said smiling with pride. "Which of course, I vow never to give you cause to call me anything other than Logan."

"Good to know—Logan," she replied, her soft smile warming his heart.

As they walked the short distance to the Dodge House, Logan pointed out various stores that he thought Rose would find interesting enough to want to frequent. "And this is the mercantile, where you'll find all manners of female necessities. I think tomorrow will be soon enough for you to find everything you need; don't you Rose?"

"Yes, yes tomorrow will be just fine."

"Daddy!" Logan turned just in time to catch Lilly in his arms. She showered him with kisses, her short cropped brown hair flopping about. "Lilly, this is Abigail. Your new mother. She's come all the way from Wisconsin to help me with the house and to help you with your school work."

Logan's heart fell when Lilly scowled at his new wife, her brown eyes filled with suspicion. "But I've got Miss Montana Sue to help me with my school work, Daddy. She loves playing, more than ciphering." Lilly gave her daddy her best pout, and an exaggerated sniff. "Why can't Miss Montana be my new momma?"

Logan looked down at his new wife, surprised at the tenderness in her gaze. "Lilly, that's a discussion for later on sweetheart. How about if we all go have a family dinner at the Dodge House? I hear they are serving veal bits, your favorite. Then we can go home and you can show your new momma where everything is in the house."

Lilly continued her scrutiny of Rose and Logan didn't like it one bit. He'd been right in finding a suitable wife and mother. While the girls at the Lady Gay were more than loving with Lilly, it was Montana Sue who had taken a shine to her. Logan liked Montana, but she wasn't what he considered mother material, not for his little girl anyway. He only hoped Mrs. Abigail Rose Granger was exactly what Lilly needed. He didn't relish giving up Rose before getting to know her a mighty bit more.

ROSE WATCHED THE young girl Logan held like a breakable package in his arms. She couldn't keep a smile from her face. Lilly was every inch the tomboy from her short cropped brown hair down to her dirty britches and dusty boots. There wasn't a darn thing wrong with it, and it was only too evident that Logan didn't mind one bit either. He clearly loved his daughter given the way he looked at Lilly and held her safely in his arms. No one was ever going to hurt Lilly as long as Logan had anything to say, or do, about it.

"Hi, Miss Granger," Rose greeted, fighting back the urge to take Lilly in her arms and shower her with love. Whoever this Montana Sue was Lilly seemed to think highly of, she'd obviously done her best to look after the girl—even if she'd rather play than do school work. Rose knew there needed to be a balance of both and she hoped to show Lilly how to accomplish that balance.

"Daddy?" Lilly asked, casting Rose a side glance.

"Yes, Lilly." Logan's gaze filled to the brim with love as he looked into his daughter's inquisitive eyes. Rose's heart sank a bit; it was all too clear there wasn't room for another. What had she expected? That once her intended had seen she was young, that he'd instantly open his heart to her? No, this was a marriage of convenience. He'd advertised for someone to manage the house and his daughter, nothing more, nothing less. No matter how much her heart pounded when he looked at her. Or how her body warmed at his touch. She'd accepted those terms, or rather, Abby had accepted those terms.

"Can we get a special treat after dinner, if I'm good?" Lilly batted her eyes at her father and Rose about burst out in laughter.

One of the things she learned from Miss Montana Sue? Rose wondered, looking away so the girl wouldn't think she was being laughed at.

"We'll see. Rose has had a long trip to get here." Logan reached down, wrapping his big, warm hand around hers. "I'm sure she'd love a bath after eating dinner. How about if you and Rose go on a shopping trip tomorrow and then stop for a treat?"

Lilly furrowed her brows, and pointedly at Rose as they stepped into the diner at the Dodge House. It was the last time Lilly even glanced at Rose for the rest of the day.

While the words of marriage passed between Logan and her, they made no sense to Rose. She said the proper things at the proper time. Even allowed her new husband to kiss her gently on the cheek at the end. Then Lilly came bounding up the street and Rose's heart melted all over again. Even at dinner as they passed the veal, roasted potatoes with gravy, and the huge basket of bread between them, confusion and apprehension filled her.

In the span of a few weeks, Miss Roseanne Duncan had become Miss Abigail Johnson, and now rode in a buckboard next to the man she'd not met until today as his wife. Rose Duncan was now Mrs. Abigail Rose Granger—wife and mother. But as she'd used a false name was their union even legal?

CHAPTER THREE

Rose woke from her exhausted sleep feeling clean and refreshed. Her hair no longer smelled of smoke, and her body had lost all its grit and grime. She'd spent the night tucked into a feather bed of fresh linens after the long, hot bath Logan had prepared for her. Since she hadn't any bed clothes, her new husband laid out one of his clean shirts for her to wear.

New husband! Oh no, I need to get up and feed my new family. Logan will think he's married a lollygagger if there's not a hot breakfast on the table for him and Lilly. Rose scampered out of bed and grabbed her only dress from the winged back chair. The calico fabric slightly damp to the touch. When she looked it over, many of the dirtiest spots were mostly gone. Sometime during the night, someone slipped in and tried to clean up her dress. She owed Logan a big show of appreciation for the kind gesture. She'd at least make him a hot, home cooked breakfast for his trouble.

When they'd arrived last night after dinner and a

brief celebration with well-wishers, the sun had already begun to set. Logan insisted Rose not worry about anything other than a hot bath and a good night's rest. There would be plenty of time for her to explore the house in the morning. She'd gladly accepted his suggestion and followed Lilly up the winding stairs to her bedroom. Lilly would sleep in the room across from hers, while Logan had the larger one in the front. As tired as she was, Rose was thankful her husband kept his word of separate sleeping arrangements.

Soon after she'd gotten Lilly settled into bed, which Rose found refreshing when there was no resistance. Logan began lugging steamy buckets of water up the stairs for her bath. Rose had slipped off her travel weary garments, then tested the water and submerged herself in its warmth. Within her reach lay a bar of soap and a sponge. A drying towel lay across the wedding knot quilt on her bed.

That was last night, her wedding night, sleeping alone in an unfamiliar bed. A quick ping of regret and semblance of loss touched her heart. It wasn't exactly how she'd pictured her most beloved day, but given her circumstances had accepted the terms. Convenience and necessity—not love.

"Enough self-pity, Rose. You've a family to feed." Rose wiped away the tear sliding down her face then slipped into her fresh smelling dress. There was only one person who could have taken the time to make sure she had something halfway presentable to wear today when she went into town. She walked over to the pitcher and bowl, splashed some water on her face, then ran wet fingers through her hair before pulling it back with a ribbon. She crept quietly out of her room and down the stairs, straight into the kitchen slowing along the way as she passed through the dining room.

The room was sparsely furnished with a table big enough to feed a family of six, large matching chairs placed haphazardly around it. The wood looked dark and expensive at one time, but now was worn and well used. Grey tinged curtains hung in the window, badly in need of some scrubbing. *Were these things his previous wife had picked out for their home? Or had all the household items and furniture come with the house when Logan purchased it?*

"Ah, there she is. Good morning, Rose." Logan warmly smiled, leaning against the door frame with the coffee pot in his hand. "Do you drink coffee?"

"Yes, with a bit of milk and sugar. Are you ready for breakfast?" Rose answered surveying the room. It was still plenty early as the sun hadn't fully risen above the eastern horizon. "Where's Lilly? I'm sorry I overslept."

Logan chuckled, pouring the rich smelling, copper liquid into a cup of fine porcelain. "Lilly was up and out the door before I could get my boots on. She said Montana was waitin' on her this morning. Something about practicing her numbers and letters."

Disappointment ebbed through Rose. "I'm sorry to have missed her. I was looking forward to our shopping trip into town this morning." Picking up the cup, she blew at some of the billowing steam. "I don't mean to pry, but don't you think it's a might early for her to be going into town alone? Did she have something to eat before she left? School hasn't started, has it?" *Was there even a school? I didn't see one, or hear anyone mention a schoolmarm.*

"No, there's no school today. I'm sure she'll be eating with Montana; the woman spoils her to no end." Logan chuckled lightly for a moment before his face turned serious. "I didn't think about her going alone, I'm so used to her doing chores in the house and going to the mercantile for me. I almost missed her as it is. She was in a hell fire hurry this morning." Logan pursed his lips, a thought crossing the surface of his eyes. "Lilly's usually not the rise and shine kind of girl, she's so used to my late nights at…"

Logan looked at Rose, his tanned face suddenly gone pale. By the way he turned away, he was keeping something from her. So far, their marriage of convenience was adding more and more deception to it. If their life together was already packed with lies, what would the future hold for them?

Before Rose could ask him what he meant to say, Logan looked at her a grin playing at the corners of his mouth. "How about if you and I go into town? I'll collect Lilly and we can get some breakfast at the Dodge House, then shop for the things you need here. I'm sure you could use a few new dresses; some female items you need. I know the pantry will need to be stocked. We are plum out of Indian meal for Johnny Cakes in the morning."

"I'd like to make some gingerbread for supper when we get back," Rose suggested glancing in the cupboards for the ingredients. "Looks like we'll need lard and molasses. It might be best to let Lilly be with Miss Montana this morning. She has a lot to figure out, even for a little girl. Yesterday when she woke it was just her and her daddy. Now today she's got a momma she doesn't know. That's a lot to take on all at once for someone so young."

"Why Mrs. Granger, you are a wise woman." Logan smiled and held the kitchen door open, waiting for her. "Then I think we'd better go before Collar's runs out of everything you need."

"Well, if you'd been better at keeping a well-stocked kitchen..." Rose scowled, then laughed realizing he was kidding with her. With Logan's hand at her elbow, they headed down the back steps and across the yard to the waiting buckboard.

EXCEPT FOR THE sound of the horses clip clopping and wheels of the wagon crunching the pitted road, the short mile ride into town was quiet. Logan glanced over at his new wife, not quite believing the lovely, young woman had his name. He'd been prepared for an average woman several years his senior. Had resolved himself to living a loveless life, with an honorable woman to care for Lilly. Instead he got Rose, as Abigail preferred to be called, a few years his junior and full of life by the looks of her.

There was a spark in her brown eyes that mesmerized him. She could ask him for anything and he'd find a way to give it to her. Damn! He had a school boy's crush on the new girl in town, who happened to be his new wife. His heart would be in trouble if he didn't stick to their marriage agreement.

Last night after he'd gotten them all home and the bath ready for Rose, he retired to the library mulling things over. He'd never thought he'd take on another wife, but he'd done just that. And a right pretty one at that. How in the world was he going to live up to his promise of keeping to his own room when all he wanted was to take Rose in his arms every time he looked at her?

Hours and a few sips of whiskey later the house had grown quiet. Logan crept up the stairs and peeked in on Lilly as he did every night before retiring to his lonely bed. His little girl slept like an angel, her doll that had once been Katie's, safely under the covers with her.

Without giving it a second thought, he found himself standing in Rose's door, watching her sleep. The moonlight glistened off her dark, golden hair. A breeze coming through the window played with a few stray strands. She was as beautiful asleep as she was awake.

There was so much trust in her relaxed features, he questioned why he didn't send her back. She'd obviously lied in her answer to his advertisement. Abigail Rose Johnson Granger was *not* a matronly woman looking for a bit of adventure in the west. She was here now and he wouldn't, couldn't, send her away. How was he going to break it to her he was a barkeep at the Lady Gay, one of Dodge's many saloons?

Lies, lies, and more lies.

"Daddy." Lilly tugged at his pant leg, her ragged old cloth doll snug in her arms. "Does Miss Rose have other clothes to wear?"

"No honey, she doesn't." Logan scooped her up in his arms, then quietly shut Rose's door. He brushed Lilly's mussed hair from her face and gazed into her sleepy eyes. "You should be in bed. It's late sweetheart, and you need to get some sleep. The sun will be up before you know it."

"But Daddy," Lilly protested, sliding out of Logan's arms and into her small bed. "Her dress is so dusty. You always tell me that cleanliness is next to Godliness after I get my britches dusty, dirt on my hands, and mud on my face when I been wrestlin' with Bobby James. Isn't it the same for Miss Rose?"

Logan gazed down at his daughter with tenderness and tucked the coverlet around her small body. "Yes Lilly, it is true. I tell you that all day, every day it seems. Rose, your momma, traveled a long way to get here so she could look after you. She wasn't able to bring any of her other dresses with her, that's why she doesn't have a clean one."

Lilly yawned, rolling onto her side. "Then Miss Rose needs to git clean to be next to God, Daddy."

Pride swelled Logan's heart. He'd not taken into consideration his new wife might not take a hankering to putting a soiled dress on after a bath. It took a soon to be six-year-old to remind him of the needs of a woman.

He'd crept into Rose's room, taking her faded blue calico dress down to the washtub for a good scrubbing. Now, sitting beside her, he was mighty pleased with the results. Rose looked totally refreshed when she'd come down this morning. The ease of those first moments gone as they drove into town. She kept her hands folded on her lap, her face etched in thought.

"Logan." Rose's voice rose above the wagon's creaking. "You haven't told me what type of work you do, or anything about you and Lilly. I know I've only been here less than a day, but I think it's important for me to know so I can begin to understand Lilly."

"Whoa." Logan swallowed hard, pulling the only two horses he owned to a halt.

Tying them off, he turned to Rose, taking her hands in his own. The small gold band on her ring finger smooth against his skin, not unlike the feel of her hand in his. Soft, dainty, and cold. *Cold hands, warm heart*, he reminded himself.

"There's not much to tell really. You already know about Lilly, she's the reason I sent for a wife. I needed someone to look after her and make sure she grows up into a lovely, educated woman." Logan recited the needs listed in his search for a bride. He knew they weren't what Rose wanted; it was all he was willing to tell her for now.

"Yes, but while that is true, what of her momma?" Rose looked into Logan's eyes and his heart slammed against his chest. Her questions were multiplying. He needed to tell her enough until they got into town where she may be distracted for a few hours. He'd deal with any other questions tonight, as they sat by the fire after dinner.

"Katie died from scarlet fever before our fifth year as man and wife. Lilly was only four years old then, she'll be six on the fourteenth of next month." Logan was surprised by the sadness, the emptiness, that still flowed in his heart and soul. He'd thought after two years the memory of Katie's loss would have subsided. Rose asking only made the still waters begin to trickle again.

"I'm sorry for your pain, Logan. I can tell how much you miss her." Rose put a hand over his, squeezing it lightly. There was compassion in her words, not pity. "I can tell you are an educated man. How is it you and your daughter live in a town with the reputation Dodge City has? Are there any schools here for children her age to attend? The streets are reportedly lined with wranglers and gunfighters. Not to mention the saloon girls and their—talents."

Logan stifled the urge to laugh out loud. Her description of Montana Sue's line of work made it sound like a soiled profession. In some ways, Rose was right. But not all the girls at the Lady Gay were soiled doves. A few, like Montana, were only trying to survive.

"Yes, I do have an education from one of the finest law schools in the country. I was a lawyer in Chicago for a few years, but after Katie died—I wanted a fresh start far from that life." Logan picked up the reins, urging the horses forward. He really needed to tell Rose everything. Well, almost everything in his own way and time. First would be about the Lady Gay, before someone else came forth with the information and had Rose thinking he was a gambling man, or worse a drunk.

"We'll miss Etta May's Johnny Cakes, fried potatoes, and the best curried bacon in town if we don't get a movin'."

There was no reason for her to know about his

THE RELUCTANT BRIDE
(Brides Along the Chisholm Trail)

undercover work with the Pinkerton Agency at this point. No sense in giving his young wife cause to worry so soon. He still had to discover what was happening to the Kennedy cattle on the drives from Texas to the livestock trains in Dodge.

"I HOPE I can change your mind one of these mornings about Etta May's being the best place for breakfast." Rose said as Logan pulled up at Wilson's Livery. Rose about jumped from the buckboard as he lifted her down.

Etta May's was only a few buildings from the livery, yet with the weaving and dodging they had to do before stepping up on the wooden walkway it took several minutes to arrive. The sooner they got over to the restaurant the better. Rose needed a good hardy breakfast if she was going to visit the proper establishments for the items her new home required. She always did her best thinking while doing the household marketing, and she had a number of things to ponder.

Had Rose made the right choice in taking Abby's place here? Yes, she was far from the reaches of that leach Griswold, but at what cost? She'd barely had time to say goodbye to her family, and by now she was sure her mother had already sobbed a river of tears. Rose prayed one day she'd be able to live up to her written promise to her mother, and write a letter detailing her new life.

And what of Abby? The thoughts of what lies she'd told on Rose's behalf was worrisome. Between the two of them, they'd worked it out that Rose would go do the marketing the day she had to leave and not return.

There'd be no note left behind, nothing to indicate where she might have gone or why. Abby would box all her clothes, sending them to her family and keeping a few items Rose had designated to be sent once it was safe.

How long would it take for her to be safe? Had she put this man and his young daughter in harm's way by coming here?

"I will certainly give you that opportunity as many mornings as you wish." Logan chuckled, taking a firm grasp of her elbow and guiding her through the horses, buggies, and townsfolk roaming town.

"Huh, oh yes, competing with Etta May's for breakfast. I do plan on winning, you know." Rose pushed her fearful thoughts back to their hiding places. Glancing down the street again she saw Lilly running as fast as her pant covered legs would carry her along the wooden planked walk. It was a reminder that Rose had bigger things that needed tending to. One of which was showering this little girl with as much love as she could.

"Daddy!" Lilly ran up to Logan, throwing her arms around his hips.

"You and I will have a talk about leaving for town so early." Logan scolded lightly, then smoothed his large hand tenderly over the girl's hair. "Now, shouldn't you say good morning to Rose as well?"

Lilly looked up at Rose her smile wavering. "Good morning, Miss Rose."

Rose knelt down to Lilly's level. "Good morning, Lilly. I'm sorry that I missed you this morning."

"Oh that's all right," Lilly pulled at an ear, pushing her short hair back. "Miss Montana was awaitin' for me."

Rose's heart pinched a bit. It was obvious the girl had some feelings for Montana Sue, and Rose understood that. The woman has been looking after her for Logan for God knew how long, and now that Rose was here—well it would take some time for everyone to adjust.

"She was? Where is she now, Lilly? I'd like to meet this lady you are so fond of." Rose smiled, glancing up and down the walk half expecting to see the woman in question racing to keep up. "She must be a very special lady."

"Oh she's got things to do. Told me to head on up to Etta May's as my daddy would be there soon enough, and she was right!" Lilly slipped her hand into Logan's pulling him into the restaurant. "Come on, Daddy, I'm hungry."

Logan laughed, the grin on his face as wide as the prairie. "Well, then let's get some cakes and Etta May's fancy sauce for them."

Rose followed as father and daughter, hands held, arms swinging, stepped into Etta May's. There was a tremendous amount of love marching in front of her. How in God's name would she fit in?

Rose immediately felt welcomed the moment she stepped through the doors. The little eatery was plainer than the Dodge House, and much homier. The smell of brown sugar and bacon frying, rich coffee brewing, and the banging of pots and pans from the kitchen would make even a hardened criminal feel he was in his mamma's home. Maybe that's why it felt like she'd walked into the kitchen back home.

Abby, I'm so sorry. Rose's guilt threatened her sensibilities once more. *No! Abby sent me here for more than to save me from Griswold.*

"Look Daddy, our favorite table right by the windows is empty." Lilly ran over to the table hopping into one of the two chairs. Pushing a lock of hair out of her face, Lilly peered out the window watching Dodge come fully awake.

She's forgotten there are three of us. Rose picked at her bottom lip with her teeth. What if she doesn't want Rose there? Will Logan send her away and look for a woman more suitable? Rose looked up at her husband, his eyes expressing little concern. Maybe she was only imagining things. When he turned to her, a small smile at the corners of his mouth, her heart pounded. Warmth radiated through her body. Logan hadn't forgotten about her.

Logan knelt beside Lilly, her little hand in his massive one. "We need a table for three now. How about if we take that one near the piano? You can still look out the window and watch everyone like always."

Rose placed a hand on Logan's shoulder, every muscle in her quivering. If what she was about to suggest didn't work, then she'd have lost this one little attempt for Lilly to feel at ease with her in their lives. "How about if I see if I can pull up a chair instead. If this is Lilly's favorite table, then it should continue to be."

Logan stood, a toothy smile spreading across his face. "That's a great idea. Let me get a chair, there are so few people here I'm sure Miss Etta won't mind one bit.

And I'll give them our order as well. Shall I order three of everything?"

Rose nodded, but her heart filled with dismay. Lilly sat staring at her with her mouth pinched together, her brow furrowed. Something big was on this little girl's mind. Rose had a feeling it had something to do with her.

"Miss Rose?" Lilly's little blue eyes squinted at her.

"Yes, Lilly."

"Why did you come here to marry my daddy? Do you love 'em?" Lilly asked in the matter-of-fact way all children ask questions.

Unsure of how to answer, Rose sighed. "It's a long story that I think only your daddy can answer, Lilly. I think your daddy is a wonderful man, and he cares for you very much. We've only just met, and sometimes love is something that grows like a flower in the spring."

"I heard Miss Montana tell Bessie that you stole him." Lilly gazed out the window, her expression going from accusatory too soft and angelic. "Miss Montana loves my daddy, she told me so this morning."

Rose's breath hitched in her throat. There was a woman in town who actually loved Logan. Why didn't he marry her, rather than send away for a bride? It made no sense, none at all.

Taking a deep breath, Rose sat back in her chair. "I really don't know Lilly. Have you asked your daddy why…"

"Asked me why what?" Logan set the chair between them. His face edged with concern, he placed two full coffee cups and a glass of milk on the table.

Lilly's eyes widened with fear, her gaze darting between her father and Rose.

"Whether or not Lilly will be able to help me make gingerbread tonight." Rose lied. She wasn't about to put a wedge between a little girl and her father for her own foolish pride.

Logan's smile was bright. "I think that might be arranged, if you two ladies can find everything you need at the mercantile."

Lilly dug into her Johnny cakes smothered in butter and rich syrup, bacon sandwiched between them. Logan drank his coffee, cutting his daughter's food for her when she couldn't. The chatter between father and daughter was light and cheery, nothing of any significance.

As they sat finishing their first breakfast as a family, Rose wondered about Logan and Lilly's relationship. Just how much time had this six-year-old girl been spending with a woman named Montana Sue? What kind of a name was that for a respectable nanny? Did Miss Montana Sue do more than watch after Lilly, is that why she was in love with Logan? Whoever Montana Sue was she plainly had Lilly on her side, and Rose wasn't exactly sure how she felt knowing another woman had desires for her husband.

CHAPTER FOUR

"That was the best breakfast in town. Thank you, Logan for bringing me here. And thank you, Lilly, for having breakfast with me during your busy morning." *With the woman who says she loves your daddy*, Rose wanted to add aloud rather than in her thoughts. *What do you expect. The woman's been here for both of them, while you're a runaway from justice. At least the woman tells the truth, whereas you're frightened to face it.*

Did Logan know there was an available woman right here in Dodge City who had feelings for him? Someone who probably knew Lilly as a mother should, and not a complete stranger with no experience except her own siblings. *He must know, otherwise he wouldn't have sent for me if the feelings were mutual. Remember he chose you! No, he chose Abigail. I'm an impostor with nowhere to run. He kept you, said you suited him just fine.*

Rose grasped Logan's hand, holding it a moment longer than necessary. Her hand tingled when he squeezed and smiled down at her.

"It was my pleasure to have both my ladies at my side." Logan began humming a tune sounding very much like *Yellow Rose of Texas*, as the three of them strolled down the walk and over to Collar's general store.

Across the street in front of the barbershop a man sat back in a chair, a booted foot propped leisurely against the hitching rail. His white beard appeared unkempt and in need of a trim at the very least.

A big bay horse passing in front of the man drew Rose's gaze upward. The man sitting in the saddle glanced her way, his black jacket tucked behind the silver studded holster strapped to his hip. His glaze was icy even as he tipped his hat then rode on. In that brief moment, Rose wasn't sure whether or not to be afraid.

"That's Bat Masterson," Logan said in a low voice as he leaned in closer to Rose. "He must be in town to see his brothers. Ed rode out this morning, but Jim is down at the Lady Gay. I'm guessing he's headed that way."

Rose watched the well-dressed man as he rode down Front Street, his head swiveling from side-to-side. She noticed the few patrons on the walks gave notice to his presence for a moment, then went back to their morning business. Even the horses hitched along the street seemed to have moved, making room for him and the big bay to pass.

Rose dismissed the man and continued to window shop, noticing the merchandise displayed were less about women's necessities and more about what one

THE RELUCTANT BRIDE
(Brides Along the Chisholm Trail)

would find in the kitchen or barn. There wasn't a lady's hat on display in any of the windows let alone a dress or two. Only harnesses, bags of flour, ammunition, medicines of all kinds—hardly anything to suit a woman's fancy.

"Logan, good to see you!" A young, clean shaven man with dark unruly hair bellowed out as they walked through the doors of Collar's. Rose guessed the store clerk to be in his early twenties, not much younger than her twenty-two years. "This must be the misses. I heard you went and got yourself married." The store clerk tugged at his striped vest then drew a long stick of peppermint from a glass jar, offering it to Lilly, which she snatched as soon as Logan gave her the nod to accept the sweet gift.

"Toby, this is my new bride, Abigail Granger." Logan introduced her, and the hint of pride in his words drew her attention from the rows of canned goods and bolts of cloth. "Abigail, this here is Toby Harvey."

"Ma'am, welcome to Dodge City." Toby tipped his head, the smile broad and friendly, matched his laughing eyes. Rose liked him instantly.

"Please, call me Rose, it's my middle name you see." Rose added when Mr. Harvey looked at her with confusion.

"Toby, please extend Rose all the credit she needs. I'm afraid the kitchen pantry is a bit sparse and in need of several dry goods." Logan chuckled, moving Lilly away from the peppermint jar. "I'll settle up with you in a few days. One is more than enough, Lilly."

Toby nodded, pulling out a book to write down

Rose's purchases as she pulled a few containers of molasses from a shelf. "Logan, didn't you say cornmeal was needed for Johnny cakes? I'd like to start my persuasion of keeping both you and Lilly home for breakfast each morning." Rose smiled, confident she had the proper cooking skills to indeed keep not only Lilly's belly filled, but also her husband's. There'd be no need for them to venture into town to eat as long as they have provisions—and her cooking was edible enough as to not send them gagging and running out the door.

Logan's laugh was deep and rumbling, "That is a bet I'll take Mrs. Granger."

Rose blushed, a rush of heat surging through her cheeks. She lowered her lashes and looked away walking over to the rows of bolted cloth. She touched several, yearning to grab them up as well. The cloth would be a luxury she wasn't sure Logan could manage on credit. Besides, she had a perfectly good dress she could wear as long as it didn't get too dirty, and there was a sewing box in the house for mending. Logan slid in from behind, his hand smooth over her digits caressing the cotton calico material.

"I think this blue color will look good on you," he whispered in her ear, sending waves of heat through her inner core. "Toby, add at least five bolts of cloth to my bill, whichever Rose would like."

Rose continued inspecting the cloth, choosing a soft paisley for both her and Lilly, a small bolt of satin to use for frills, some colored ribbons for trim, and finally the bolt of blue calico Logan fancied. She also purchased several items of dry and canned goods she'd written

THE RELUCTANT BRIDE
(Brides Along the Chisholm Trail)

down. She chanced a glance at Logan as he talked with Toby about horses, the cattle coming into town, and the latest rumblings about the Indian Wars.

For the first time in twenty-four hours Rose was finally getting a good look at her husband. Logan Granger stood about six foot with dark, thick hair. His eyes always kind and friendly, with a touch of sadness. A set of dimples appeared whether he smiled or laughed. His voice supported an easy drawl to it she couldn't quite define. He carried the conversation with Toby effortlessly and in a manner that was easy. It was the way he carried himself which made Rose wonder why he'd come to Dodge City and not stayed near his family after his wife passed away. There was so much they needed to discuss if they were going to get on with each other. Maybe eventually she'd be able to tell him who she truly was, and why she ran away.

Today was not the day to play the game of truths though. She wanted to know how much she could trust him not to send her on the first train back, or worse, turn her in to the marshal.

The door swept open, chasing the indoor shadows into corners. "Granger, I thought I might find you here since Etta told me you brought your family to town," Deputy Marshal Hawkins stood in the door, his large frame blocking the morning light. "Can you come over to the office, there's something I need to speak to you about. Marshal Jones rode out on personal business this morning."

"Sure thing, Deputy." Logan glanced over at Rose, his face suddenly sullen. "Rose, I'll meet you back at

Etta May's when you and Lilly are finished. Make sure you both get some ice cream while you are there as well."

Rose watched as Logan ambled out of Collar's on the heels of Deputy Marshal Hawkins.

"MISS ROSE?" LILLY'S tiny voice held a slight tremble.

Rose looked down at Lilly as her new daughter stared at her father walking out the door with the deputy marshal. When Lilly turned her ghostly gaze to Rose, worry flashed in the pair of innocent overly bright brown eyes.

"You worried about your daddy?" Rose knelt down next to Lilly, taking her tiny hand in hers.

"Yes…ma'am." The words came out in quick bursts of breaths. Lilly's normal angelic glow now a pale gray.

"There's nothing to be concerned about, Lilly. He's with Deputy Marshal Hawkins. Besides, I have a feelin' your daddy can take care of himself." Rose smiled, chasing away her fear as well as hoping she did the same for Lilly. If only she'd believe her own words, maybe Lilly would as well. It wasn't every day that a man of the law came in asking your husband to follow him to the jail house. At least not as far as Rose was concerned, this being her first encounter with the situation and a husband. And her being well—she knew what she was. Had the marshal heard of her flight from justice?

"What if he leaves like momma did?" Lilly's bottom lip quivered and she wiped a hand across her eyes.

THE RELUCTANT BRIDE
(Brides Along the Chisholm Trail)

Rose reached out to take Lilly in her arms, but she drew away. Rose's heart ached for the little girl. "He's going to meet us at Etta May's after we've gotten all the provisions to stock the pantry. And he suggested that we get some ice cream while we wait. Would you like that?"

Lilly's eyes brightened, and she nodded her head with enthusiasm. "Can I help?"

"Of course you can help. I'd very much appreciate it." Rose smiled warmly, feeling the rush of a small acceptance from the girl. Even if it was the thought of ice cream that chased Lilly's fear away, Rose was thankful for the offer.

Lilly wandered over to the bags of potatoes and flour giving them the once over when the door swung open. Looking up she rushed into the skirts of a woman. "Miss Montana! Daddy had to go with Deputy Marshal Hawkins."

Rose's heart fell to the floor, its final beats of life fading away. The woman was as close too beautiful as Rose would admit. Her shiny rich brown hair piled on her head in a neat and orderly fashion, with ear bobs dangling from the lobes. The yellow satin and lace gown made Rose's travel worn calico shabby in contrast. The satin waist cinched in to the perfect hour glass shape. Rose absently ran her hands over her own waistline in comparison.

So this is the woman who loves Logan. He could do worse I suppose. Rose stood there a moment gathering her wits about her. Taking a deep breath to steady her nerves she walked over to Montana Sue, extending her hand. "Hello, I've heard so much about you from Lilly, I feel I already know you."

Montana Sue held her hand steadily against Lilly's back, as if she were protecting her from harm. "I can't say the same of you."

Rose withdrew her hand, and smoothed her old faded peach calico skirt. *So that's how it's going to be then.* "I'm so sorry, I should introduce myself. I'm Abigail Johnson, well, Mrs. Logan Granger now. But please, call me Rose, it's my middle name."

Montana Sue's eyebrow arched as her inspection of Rose started at the worn toe of her shoes to the top of her freely hanging blond hair. A small laughing smile emerged and she patted Lilly on the back, sending her off.

"So, you are the woman Logan sent away for." Montana Sue swayed into the room, her satin skirts rustling just above the dusty wooden floors of the store. "I'd heard something about why he hadn't been to work last night at the Lady Gay. I wouldn't believe he was fool enough to send away for a mail order bride, and someone from outside of Dodge City at that."

The Lady Gay? That's where Logan said Bat Masterson was riding to this morning. Logan works there? As what? She felt like a fool being caught off guard this way. He'd made her think he was a prosperous businessman. She endeavored to hide her shock not wanting to give Montana Sue any more ammunition to use against her.

She raised a brow refusing to rise to the bait even though they echoed her sentiments when Abby mentioned the idea. "Yes, he's married a woman outside of Dodge City. In fact, I'm from Wisconsin where I helped manage a rather large household," Rose said with pride, defending herself for whatever reasons were unknown to her. What did she have to prove to this woman in the first place? That she was more worthy of being Logan's wife and Lilly's mother than Montana Sue?

Montana Sue continued to saunter around Collar's touching a few female trinkets, sniffing bottles of perfume here and there. "Yes, well be that as it may. It must be difficult to marry a man who doesn't know you. For that matter, who in fact doesn't even love you. I mean, how could he? He doesn't have a notion who you are. I know I couldn't do it, no matter the reasons or the temptations."

Rose caught herself tapping a booted toe in frustration, then immediately quit. She wasn't sure if she should ignore the unpleasant underhanded accusations, or have a shootout with the impetuous woman. Oh, this woman was starting to get under her skin and she hardly knew her. What was it her mother said about women? Oh yes, keep your friends close but your rivals closer— or something like that. Well, Montana Sue definitely fell into the rival category.

Rose approached the counter where Toby had all but plastered himself against the shelves. "Toby, I think Lilly and I have completed our shopping for today. Can you please have these things ready for when Logan and I return home in an hour or so?"

Toby swallowed hard, noting the items on the credit slip. His previously neat writing no more than scribbling now. "Yes ma'am. They'll be ready when Mr. Granger comes for them."

"Thank you Toby, and please call me Rose." Rose smiled, then gathered her faded skirt in her hand. "Lilly, are you ready for that ice cream?"

Lilly ran over to Montana Sue hugging her skirts once more, then she scurried out the door ahead of Rose. Rose turned to Montana Sue, giving her the best smile she could. "Good day, and it was a pleasure meeting you. I hope we become fast friends."

Rose turned and followed in Lilly's wake, every muscle in her body feeling like rubber.

#

"WHAT'S THIS ALL about, Gabe?" Logan asked feeling he left Lilly at the opening of an angry bee's hive. He'd noticed Montana Sue making her way up the walk, her head held high and a snap in her step. "Hope it doesn't take too long, Montana Rose is headed for Collar's." *I hope Rose can hold her own against Montana when she's got that look about her.*

"Sorry to drag you away from the misses, Logan. I know you've got your hands full with your new wife and Montana, but if it wasn't important I'd have left you there for the boxing match." Gabe Hawkins chuckled, his hands loose and level with the pearl handles of his six shooters hanging from his hip. "Some brand altering information came into the office I think you might want to look over."

"The Double K, again?" Logan had been close more times than he cared to admit in the past few months in catching the rustlers of the Kennedy cattle.

THE RELUCTANT BRIDE
(Brides Along the Chisholm Trail)

Each drive, old Cyrus Kennedy reported he'd lost at least another dozen or so head by the time they got to Dodge. Only Marshal Jones and Deputy Marshal Hawkins were privy as to what Logan's main purpose in town was, and it wasn't only to be the barkeep at the Lady Gay. It was to gather as much information as possible, and then put the rustlers in jail for good.

Once this assignment was done, he'd sell the house and furniture, pack up his family, and head straight back to Chicago where there was a bit of civilization and good schools for Lilly. Now with Rose in the picture, she'd be closer to her family as well. Maybe they'd make a trip up to Helena and see his ma and pa before heading back to the city, if the season were right. Winters in Montana could be brutal for anyone traveling by stage or wagon. Many froze to death after the animals did.

"Cyrus Kennedy sent a telegram saying he was riding along with the next herd. Here tell, he's got a hired gun riding with his drovers now." Gabe pushed open the door, then strolled over to the coffee pot sitting on the cook stove. "I think it's a fool thing for the man to do, but it's his cattle."

Logan followed Gabe into the marshal's office and took a seat near to the door. He wanted to keep an eye on Collar's in case a hissy fight broke out and he needed to throw some water on a couple of wild cats. If that didn't work, then he'd have the deputy marshal throw them both in jail to cool their heels for the night. He'd deal with the aftermath of it in the morning.

"No thanks, I'll pass for now," Logan waved off the cup offered to him. "I don't need the jitters from that stuff. When did Kennedy say the herd was leaving?"

"In a few days, and with both the marshal and Ed out of town—well, I thought it best I gave you the information seeing as how you're a Pinkerton." Gabe slammed down the coffee, his face grimacing as it slid down his throat. "Damnable stuff. I need someone who can make a good pot of this sludge."

"Maybe you ought to get yourself a mail order bride, Gabe." Logan suggested, knowing full well that was the last thing Gabe Hawkins would do seein' as how he liked being free and easy. Just because Logan was more than pleased with the one he'd married last night, he doubted Gabe would find him a bride as fine as Rose.

As far as Logan was concerned, he'd gotten the best hand dealt out in the mail order bride deal. He pondered his luck. While Rose would definitely be passingly pretty to some, she was beautiful in his eyes. Her golden hair drawn back and falling free around her shoulders and back. Even her faded calico dress looked every bit as fetching as she did. She had an easy way with Lilly, and while Rose was proper in a leisurely way, it suited him just fine. Yep, he'd won the high stakes in that card game.

In less than twenty-four hours Abigail Rose Johnson Granger had gotten under his skin.

"I don't know how you could do it with a job like yours. But I know you've got Lilly to think about, and raisin' her right. Workin' as a Pinkerton is as dangerous as being marshal, I suspect." Gabe pulled up a chair across from Logan, a smirk across his weather lined face. "That new wife of yours sure is mighty pretty, that much I'll give you. And suspicious. She would hardly have a conversation with me in the train on the way down from Topeka. I almost split a gut when she told me in her snooty manner that she was going to Dodge City to marry the prosperous Mr. Granger!"

Logan looked across the street and grimaced. "I was pretty vague in my letters, only that I needed someone to care for Lilly and the house. I surely didn't expect Rose though."

Gabe sat back in his chair, his silence anything but comforting. "Now that we know Kennedy is with his herd, keep your ears perked. If one of those drunken cowpokes in town says anything, let me handle it. You've got a wife and a child to look after."

Logan smiled seeing Rose and Lilly walk out of Collars in one piece. "Thanks for the information, Gabe. I think I'm going to go have some dessert with my daughter and new wife."

Logan headed out the door, Gabe's deep rumbling laughter following him.

CHAPTER FIVE

THE SWEET AROMA of fresh baking apples filled the kitchen. Rose watched as her family ate the meager dinner she'd prepared with vigor. Lilly's tongue snaked out snatching a bit of sauce from the baked beans settled in the corner of her mouth. Logan sopped up his bean juice with the corn bread she and Lilly made earlier.

"Almighty Rose, if you keep cooking like this I won't be able to walk again." Logan sat back, rubbing his hands over his stomach. "Best darn meal I've had in years."

Rose snorted, turning away so Logan didn't see her amusement. This simple fare was nothing compared to the meals her former employers ate but it was the best she could come up with on the spur of the moment. "If beans, potatoes, and cornbread are the best you've eaten then I wonder what you've been eating all this time."

"I ain't never had 'tatoes like these before." Lilly mumbled her compliment over a last mouthful of potatoes. "Miss Montana's not gonna believe this,

THE RELUCTANT BRIDE
(Brides Along the Chisholm Trail)

Daddy."

Rose's soaring heart took a nose dive straight into the pot she set on the cook stove. *Time Rose, give it time to erase those thoughts of being with Montana Sue from Lilly's mind. Besides, nasty as the woman acted toward you she still filled a need for this child and you can't begrudge her that. It will take time to earn Lili's affection. You've only been here for a day for pity-sake.* She grabbed a towel, opened the stove then lifted the *Bird's-nest Pudding* out. She poured some cream into a pot and set it next to the pudding too warm from the stove's heat.

Rose went to the window and stared across the yard watching the sun set in the western horizon forcing herself to relax. As wild as this place was it could still be beautiful. She mustn't let a little girl's simple comments upset her so much. She was here to do a job, not pout because a six-year-old darling who'd lost her momma at a young age slighted her. Lilly's apparent affection for the woman who had watched over her until Rose arrived was deep, and that was nothing to scorn at; she could be a bitter little girl instead of one filled with warmth and longing. Swiping at her eyes, Rose turned and put on her best smile. "There's pudding and warm cream, if you've saved room for it."

"I'll have some, but only if you'll sit with me by the fire." Logan smiled up at her with a longing in his eyes she couldn't define. It wasn't the type of a man newly married would have for his wife, it was something else she couldn't define, maybe loneliness. "Lilly can sit right where she is, and when she's done I think it's time for her to get ready for bed."

"Daddy, it's still light outside," Lilly's voice squealed across the room in protest. "I don't wanna go to bed, it's too early."

"No, it is getting dark and much later than you realize, Lilly. I have a few things to discuss with Rose tonight." Logan insisted, gathering their soiled plates and stacking them next to the sink. "I'll go out and get some water for washing these." He didn't look at either of them, just grabbed the bucket and walked out the back door.

Something weighed heavily on his mind. Did it have anything to do with the deputy marshal today? Was this the very last meal she'd ever cook for him and Lilly—her family? Pouring a bit of warm cream over a cup of the pudding, Rose shook the thoughts from her mind. Setting the cup in front of Lilly, she plopped down next to her.

"Lilly, may I ask you something?" Rose ran her hands over the old flour sack apron she'd found hanging from a peg in the pantry.

"Sure," Lilly slid a spoonful of the sweetness into her mouth, her eyes and face lighting up. "Gee, this is the best I've ever tasted Miss Rose. Even better than Etta May's or Montana Sue's. Where'd you learn to make it?"

Rose looked down into the sweet brown eyes and smiled. How could she fault this little angel for wanting to be near what was familiar to her? "Back home, from my momma. She tried to teach me all her special recipes."

"Will you teach me someday?" Lilly licked the spoon clean before dipping it back into the sweet delight. Apprehensive excitement splashed across her face at the prospect of turning apples into a pan of goodness.

"Yes, yes I will. But not until you are a bit older." Rose padded over to the stove and spooned two more cups for Logan and herself. She'd wait to top them off with the cream until Logan returned with the water, cool pudding that's meant to be warm isn't very tasty.

"What did you want to ask me, Miss Rose?" Lilly smiled at her, a pudding ring on her pink lips.

Rose's heart raced against her breast with fear. She looked away, feigning to wipe up something on the stove top. "Do you think you might one day just call me Rose instead of Miss Rose?"

"Mm-hmm." Lilly replied shoveling the last spoonful of pudding into her mouth. "Do I have to call you Momma?"

"Not if you don't want to. Rose will do just fine." Rose put up the last of their supper scrambling her brain for a recipe to use it for tomorrow's lunch.

Logan pushed his way through the back door, water slushing onto the floor. "Sorry. I decided to check on the horses and make sure they were bedded down for the night. Once I get settled in by the fire, I won't want to go back out."

Rose moved the pan and two cups of pudding onto the table, then poured cream over them. "You can put the bucket right there on the stove, it is still warm enough to heat for dish water."

Logan nodded then placed the nearly full bucket on

the stove with ease. Rose blushed as his muscles flexed under the rolled up cotton shirt sleeves. He turned, grinning, and sweet sensation floated over her. *Keep in mind he doesn't want anything more than someone to care for his daughter and his household. You'd best remember that, Rose!*

"Lilly, I don't think you need to lap up that cup and spoon like a dog!" Logan scolded his daughter, taking the items from her hands. "Now, wash up and say goodnight. And get down on your knees and say your prayers, young lady!"

Lilly's lower lip hung so low she'd have tripped over it as she walked over to the wash bowl. Splashing water on her hands and face, she said good night and trudged up the stairs, grumbling all the way.

Logan shook his head, then with warm pudding cup in hand, took a seat near the stone fireplace. "Come and sit with me Rose. The cleaning up can wait a bit longer."

ROSE PAUSED HER scrubbing the table for a moment, set the dishrag down, draped the apron over a chair, then took the chair next to him. A spoonful of pudding slid into her mouth and she gazed at him through those thick lashes of hers. Suddenly his pants got a bit snugger in places he'd nearly forgotten about.

Shoving a spoonful into his mouth, he averted his gaze from hers, least ways she'd see his building desire. "I've never had anything so delicious, not even in Chicago," Logan remarked reaching his hand over to cover hers. A spark singed the air between them.

"Thank you," Rose settled her spoon amongst the

THE RELUCTANT BRIDE
(Brides Along the Chisholm Trail)

creamy apples nestled in the cup. "Logan, I think…"

"We need to talk about Montana Sue?" Logan looked from the fire to her, a sense of chill in her otherwise friendly eyes. "Rose, I've been meanin' to—"

Losing his nerve, he looked away from her accusing gaze. How this woman had made such an impact on him in so short an amount of a time baffled him. It had taken months of courting Katie before he'd even begun to feel half of what Rose made him feel in a day.

Rose has been here twenty-four hours and all I want is to hold her close. Then kiss her the way a husband should kiss his wife…slow and tender. There are too many things that need to be said and done. The truth about my work. Montana Sue and her misguided affection. And, in good time, a proposed change in our marriage contract.

"Tell me about her? Montana Sue?"

"About that." His gaze flashed over her face and his heart ceased to beat. What in the devil happened in Collar's today? Was Rose wanting to go back to her family? Damn it! He knew he shouldn't have left the two of them alone with only Toby there to pull them apart. The poor boy probably hid in the backroom hoping any sparks didn't set the place on fire.

"Yes, please do tell me about that." Rose sighed, her face suddenly soft with curiosity. "You do know she's in love with you. Or at the very least believes she's in love with you."

"She's what?" Logan stammered, not quite sure if he'd heard Rose right. "Are you sure she said that?" He tightened the grip on the cup of pudding, denting the metal slightly. This can't be happening. When had he ever given Montana Sue a notion that he was interested in her for more than friendship?

He sensed she was telling the truth. How could he have been so blind?

"Lilly about burst at the seams telling me how sad Montana Sue was that you married another woman. At first I didn't believe that you'd shun someone so close to Lilly for a woman you knew nothing about. But there she was, in her satin dress and fancy ear-bobs, telling me how shocked she was to hear the reason you didn't show up for work at the Lady Gay was because you married some woman no one knew."

There it was out she'd told him she knew about his deception about being a businessman. He flushed with anger. Why in the world would Montana go and try to ruin his marriage? He was at the fork in the road. Did he continue the lie, accusing Montana of being a liar as well? Or come clean with the truth? He had to decide in a matter of moments what was important to him. His secret or the life he yearned for with Rose.

"I've been meaning to tell you about my job...and other things."

"I'm listening." Rose gazed at the fire, the flickering flames dancing upon her sweet face. "The woman thought you were hers, it was plain to see by the way her eyes sparked and her cheeks blushed talking about you."

Was it possible that Rose was jealous, that she was actually developing feelings for him too? It seemed too much to hope for. Logan stared at Rose, his heart cracking loudly in his chest. They had miles to go, and lots of levelling to do with each other before that could happen. "Montana Sue is a good friend. She'd been very caring and patient with Lilly from the first time we'd arrived. I didn't stop to think that she'd believe…"

"That you might love her? Yes, I see that. But she in not so many words also insinuated that you work behind the bar at the Lady Gay." Rose's chin pointed at him as if he were the worst sort of man. And he guessed she was probably right. He'd been less than truthful since she'd arrived.

Montana Sue and her attempt to run off Rose wasn't going to take root. *It's now or never. I've got to tell her the truth about the Lady Gay. And that I'm on a case undercover for the Pinkerton Agency.*

"Will you hear me out until the end?" Logan hung on to his nerve; if she took too long he'd lose it and her all in one fair swoop. "It could take all night, if you're willin' to listen. To give me a chance to say what needs to be explained." Logan wasn't one to explain anything to anyone, let alone almost begging them to listen. There was something about Rose that pulled at him. He didn't know if it was the way she looked at Lilly right off as if she were her own. Or the way she moved about preparing their meal that night, so natural like this was really her home.

"Yes Logan, I'll hear you out." Rose spoke so softly he wasn't sure if he'd heard her or not. When she looked over at him, he thought there was a glistening in her eyes. Damn, the last thing he wanted to do was cause her pain or misery.

He took a deep breath and stood near the fireplace. He needed to move out of the chair or he'd go crazy sitting. "After the war, I met Katie during Harvard law school and we wed in 1870 right after graduation. She was the daughter of the man I did some apprentice work for, and we seemed well suited for each other. Soon after we moved to Chicago where I became employed by Winston & Blodgett. It didn't take long for me to move up from petty cases to a few criminal cases that were high profile. We were happy Rose; I'd be a liar if I said otherwise.

"When Katie told me there was a baby on the way I felt my world was complete. I had a wife I adored and a little one on the way to spoil rotten. Lilly came into this world full of joy. She was a good baby, never once crying in the middle of the night." His heart swelled with love and he couldn't keep the smile from seeping onto his face.

The next part was the most difficult to talk about, even now several years later. He paced for a moment, grabbing strength to go on. He wouldn't allow that sadness to take hold of him again.

"Then Katie got sick, real sick. By the time the fever took her she wasn't my Katie any more. And I wasn't myself either. I wanted to die Rose, right along with Katie. I quit the nice, safe job at the law firm. I quickly joined the Pinkerton Agency, hoping to put myself in danger as an undercover operative. Coming to Dodge was a way for me to do that. Then one day I realized I had a little girl depending on me. Who needed me."

THE RELUCTANT BRIDE
(Brides Along the Chisholm Trail)

"...And that's all there is, Rose." Logan sat down in his chair after wearing a path across the already threadbare hearth rug. "That's everything out in the open. I've only loved one woman in my life. I don't know if one day I'd want to change our agreement. It certainly couldn't be until after I find those cattle rustlers and return to Chicago." It was next door to her hometown. Would she leave him then? Why wasn't she saying anything? She wouldn't even meet his eyes.

Logan knew if she wanted to go back to Wisconsin, he'd lose something very special he believed he'd never regain again. *Lord, I understand why you took one love from me. Please don't take another without good reason. Lilly needs a woman like Rose to help her grow into a young woman. We may never have her heart, but she's got a good start on mine.*

Rose nodded her head, her cup of pudding clenched tight in her hands, and got up from the chair. The gold band on her ring finger gleamed with the reflection of the flames, reminding him that he'd pledged to protect her. Now he hoped the truth didn't chase Rose from their lives.

ROSE SAT STARING at the fire, trying to digest everything Logan had told her. Starting with his beloved wife's death, to leaving the law firm and working for Pinkerton in hopes of joining Katie, to working undercover at the Lady Gay. He'd explained the reason he'd come to Dodge City, having been assigned to find the men rustling cattle coming up from Texas. His job at the Lady Gay gave him the opportunity to ferret out information from drunk cowpokes, and to keep his ear open to talk about the cattle drives.

Rose turned and looked into Logan's shadowed gaze. She placed the cup she'd been clenching tightly on the table next to the discarded dishrag, his words echoing through her mind. *"I've only loved one woman in my life. One day I'll love another I suppose, but not until after I find those cattle rustlers and return to Chicago."* Fearing he'd see the tears welling in her eyes, she walked slowly up the stairs to her room without looking back. She knew she should have said something. Should have run to him to try and ease his pain. She had no right to do so; it took all her will to not go against her word of no emotional connection. She was his wife in name only, there'd never be a place for her in his heart.

Reaching the top landing, she put a trembling hand to her heart. The man she was married to needed her and she had to walk away from any feelings of love toward Logan. At least she didn't have to walk away from Lilly. She stood at Lilly's bedroom door, looking in on her before going to her own room. The open window allowed the night breezes of a spring night to fill the small space. Lilly lay under the quilt, puffing short breaths of air, her rag doll tucked safely in her arms, totally unaware of the turmoil rolling through both her daddy and Rose. Rose never imagined this sweet little girl she'd never known before could make her feel so much love and yearning. Swiping away a tear, she retired to her own room. She had so much to sort out. To think about. To worry about.

Rose slipped out of her day dress and into the

makeshift night gown she'd fashioned out of an old meal sack. Once she patterned out a dress or two for both Lilly and herself, she'd use the rest of the cloth for a proper nightdress for them both. Splashing water on her face from the pitcher and bowl, she finger-combed her hair before braiding it.

She blew out the lamp and slid into bed, pulling the covers up to her chin. It was a clear spring night, the moon full and bright. Stars twinkling like firebugs. She stared out the window, tears weeping from the corners of her eyes, and she let them escape.

Was Logan feeling as much pain as she was? He had to be with all that he'd told her. He'd truly loved his wife, Katie, before the fever illness took her from them. Rose understood his misguided desire of wanting to be with his deceased wife. She saw the lingering sorrow deep in his eyes from time-to-time. She thanked the Lord, then Mr. Pinkerton for sending Logan to Dodge City, and finally to her, even if Abby was the wife he'd first expected.

Regardless of the possible danger, she could live with his undercover life here in Dodge. With his experience in the war, Rose was confident Logan would be able to handle himself if the need called for it.

As for Lilly, he said he couldn't bear to leave her behind in Chicago, or send her to his parents' ranch in northern Montana. So Logan arranged to have a catalog house sent to Dodge City to make a home for Lilly. He'd done his best, thinking the arrangement he'd made with a couple of the Lady Gay girls to watch over Lilly while he was working, was a good plan. They'd seemed to love having her to spoil and fuss over. He'd never paid much attention to their feelings toward him or Lilly. He'd didn't think he'd ever given Montana Sue any indication that he was interested in her in a wifely way. To the best of his knowledge anyway.

He'd assured Rose he wasn't in love with Montana Sue, nor any other woman from Dodge City. When she'd looked into his eyes, there was moisture skimming the surface of his sad brown orbs. Then he'd said something she couldn't quite hope for the reasoning of it. He'd thought that he one day may want to change their marriage contract, if she was agreeable to it, but how could she take that risk if love wasn't involved?

Tears flowed unabated softly over her cheeks. Logan Granger was a Pinkerton Agent. Her husband could very likely put her in jail where she may never see Lilly again, and then send her back to testify against Mr. Griswold.

CHAPTER SIX

ROSE WOKE TO the aroma of coffee and bacon wafting through the floor vent. Panic gripped her. She'd done it again, slept past the time to prepare breakfast. Throwing back her covers, she hastily splashed water on her sleepy face, and slipped into her dress. She tidied up her hair into a braided bun at the back of her neck.

Lilly's door stood ajar and the girl's bed made in the way of a six-year-old. Rose chuckled, then trotted down the stairs and into the kitchen. Logan stood at the stove cracking an egg into a hot pan.

Any joy of the morning disappeared with the reminder of last night's conversation with Logan. Nothing had been settled between them. She'd gone to bed without telling him how she was beginning to feel. How could she after all he'd confessed? She'd waited all night for Logan to come knock on her door, telling her he'd made a mistake in sending for a mail-order bride. That he had no right to marry another when he still grieved so heavily for Katie. That he'd provide a room for her at the Dodge House until she could get on the first train heading East.

She kept telling herself it would be for the best. Rose never expected to have growing feelings for her little family. The last thing she wanted was to cause them anymore heartache than they'd already endured.

She cared for Logan and Lilly too much.

"I'm so sorry, seems I've done it again." Rose was motionless. Had Logan decided to send her back after last night? "I meant to have breakfast complete with biscuits and gravy prepared before…"

Logan smiled, and her stomach fluttered. "It was a long night. I couldn't sleep." He poured her a cup of coffee and set it on the table, motioning for her to sit.

She took a deep sniff of the rich aroma, settling her nerves a bit. There was nothing like a good cup of fresh coffee in the morning to make the day seem a bit brighter when storm clouds lingered. She spied Logan over the steaming brew.

His normally combed back hair now ruffled and unruly, making him look like he'd just taken a towel to it. His usually pressed shirt was half-tucked in looking like he'd slept in it. The complete picture had Rose's belly fluttering like a hummingbird over a flower full of nectar.

"Where's Lilly?" Rose sipped the coffee, feeling the warmth in her cheeks increase as she watched Logan's every move.

"I took her to Etta May's with a strict order not to go to the Lady Gay." Logan tipped the sizzling pan over two plates and an egg slipped easily onto each one. A few of slices of crisp bacon followed the perfect eggs. "I thought it was best given our conversation last night. There is something that needs to be settled between the two of us."

Rose felt a faint glimmer of hope in her heart, but quickly dashed it away. She braced herself for the blow she felt certain was coming. He wanted their marriage annulled, ended as if the past few days didn't exist. "If you think so. You are her father after all."

"And you Rose, you're her mother." Logan sat across from her, pushing the eggs into the bacon until the soft yolks final oozed out. "The girl needs to get used to it. And so do I."

"I thought…" Rose began, looking at Logan. His gaze was fixed on his eggs and bacon, he played with them like a child. Or a man trying to figure out how to say something important and didn't know where to start.

"I'd send you away?" When his gaze matched hers her heart did a flip-flop like a rock tumbling down a hill.

Yes, because one day you might when you find out I'm not the woman you think I am. You'll want me as far from Lilly as possible. Rose nodded afraid her voice would betray her thoughts.

"Why?" Logan ceased pushing his breakfast around the blue and white speckled plate. He sat back, his gaze fixed on hers, confusion written on his face.

"You said you may want to change our marriage contract. I took it to mean you were unhappy with me and wanted to send me back. That your love for Katie is too great, you don't have room for another."

"Unhappy with you?" Logan stood and came up

behind her, putting his hands firmly on her shoulders. "If it's one thing I'm not is unhappy with is you." He pulled her up and she turned to look into his eyes. "Katie will always hold a place in my heart, she was my first love. I need you Rose more than I could have imagined. I didn't realize it until last night, after you left without a word."

Her stomach twisted in knots, Rose thought about what his words may mean. His eyes kept searching her face, then a smile appeared at the corners of his mouth. Could Logan be happy with his decision to marry her, even if it may not last forever? If allowed, she'd live beside him and raise Lilly until he would have no choice but to send his fugitive wife away. Until that day, she'd cherish each moment as if it were her last. One day it will be once the long arm of the law caught up to her.

"The reason I want to change the contract is since you arrived on that train all I've wanted to do is, well, this." Logan crushed her to his chest, capturing her mouth with his. Rose's eyes sprung open and her body stiffened like a board.

"I'm sorry, I shouldn't have done that." He released her and a chill raced through her body. Her lips tingled with want and desire. She swallowed the lump of need in her throat and smoothed down her dress when he walked away from her.

"I, I understand Logan. You're still yearning for Katie." Rose touched her lips with the tips of her fingers, then quickly gathered up the discarded meal.

"No Rose, you haven't heard what I'm saying. It's not Katie I'm yearning for, it's you." Logan whispered near her ear, sending a sweet sensation of heat through her. She heard his footsteps retreat and her head swam in circles. She hung onto the wash basin for support. "I know you've only been here for a few days, and that the contract you agreed to didn't include falling in love. I'd like to change that contract here and now. I don't want to wait until my Pinkerton business is done. I don't want to wait until Chicago."

Rose sucked in a breath, willing the words of agreement fighting to spill out to stay hidden in her mind. She didn't want to dash any hope away that he'd keep his word. That maybe there was a trace of love in his heart again. That if she spoke, he'd stop saying what needed to be said.

"I'm not saying it's love I'm feeling in the short amount of time you've been here, but I'd like to have the right to find out what it is." Logan stood rooted near the stove, his arms hanging at his side, a look of hope on his face and in his eyes. "Rose, you've touched my heart in a way I didn't think possible ever again. Being in a mail order bride situation is tough on the man also, especially when his bride isn't what he expected. Would you agree to amend certain criteria of our agreement and let nature take its course naturally?"

"Oh Logan," Rose flew into his arms and buried her face into his shoulder. "Yes, yes I'll agree to a new contract." Was it possible that she could reveal her secret to him, that there might be true love?

"Well then, let's go into town and collect our daughter." Logan suggested, holding Rose tightly. Now that he had her, there was no way he'd let her go. Last night he thought he'd been worried she'd gone upstairs to pack the few belongings she had. He half expected to find her at the bottom of the stairs this morning, with her only pocketbook in hand, asking to go back home.

To say he was ecstatic to find her sleeping peacefully when he'd gone to wake up Lilly was like a wish come true. Rose didn't look like a woman about to leave her new husband, she looked like a woman any man would love and cherish. A woman he could love and cherish.

To say fear is a powerful thing is an understatement. That fear part of the reason he couldn't sleep. The prospect of Rose leaving them, leaving him, settled like a boulder in his gut throughout the night. When he finally admitted to himself the attraction to her, Logan knew there was only one thing to do.

Renegotiate their marriage contract now, before it was too late.

"On one condition." Rose's impish grin set his heart pounding with promise. A promise of love?

"And what might that be?" Logan wiped a tear from her cheek with the pad of his thumb. "All you have to do is ask and it's yours. You'll never want for anything, Rose. You want the moon and stars, they're yours."

"No, nothing that simple," she laughed, placing her hand over his pounding heart. "You kiss me like that again and I promise you'll never desire anyone else ever." Rose whispered pressing her body into him; he caught on fire deep in his soul.

Logan tipped her chin up and searched her eyes. A passionate fire burned in her warm brown orbs. He ached to be kissed by those flames of passion. He didn't have to be told a second time; he captured her mouth with his. Logan coaxed her to open to him, to give what she could. And she did. It was good enough for him…for now. Until trust and love became one for them he'd wait to make her fully his and his alone.

The thundering of hooves halted abruptly at the front of the house. A loud knock on the door broke them completely apart. Reluctantly, Logan released his hold from around Rose, and headed to the front door. He couldn't imagine who had come calling so early in the morning; it was only a few hours past sun up. He knew Lilly was safe at Etta May's, he'd taken her there himself as soon as the day broke.

He'd wanted some privacy when he spoke with Rose this morning. Being unsure as to whether or not she'd agree to his proposal, he didn't want Lilly to be disappointed if it had gone sour. His money had been on Rose staying, and he'd won the biggest bet of his life.

He swung open the door to find Deputy Marshal Hawkins standing on the front porch, hat in his hands. Noticing several men sat on their horses, bedrolls tied behind each cantle and hanging saddlebags bulging, Logan opened the screen door and stepped out. Something must have happened over the past few days since he'd taken some time off to get his new wife settled into their lives.

"Sorry Logan, I know it's early and you're getting use to your new wife, but can you saddle up and come with us? Seems there's a lead on some rustlers out in a gully along the Cimarron between here and Fort

Supply."

Logan turned to Rose standing behind the screen door, the smile that brightened her face a moment ago fading.

Hawkins tipped his head. "Ma'am, morning."

"Morning Deputy Marshal, would you and the boys care for some coffee there's plenty left." Rose offered, turning to go fetch the pot and cups.

"Mighty nice of you ma'am. We've got a lot of ground to cover today. I'm sure the boys would be grateful for a cup when we return though." Hawkins smiled, then turned his focused back on Logan. His face was etched with worry. He lowered his voice so only Logan could hear him. "Old Simon came stumbling in this morning sayin' he heard some drunk wrangler talking last night at the Lady Gay. The drunk was braggin' about several head of cattle hold up about a day's ride from here. Might be some of the Kennedy cattle you've been lookin' for, might not be. Either way you need to find out, and I could use an extra gun."

"Let me get some provisions. I take it we'll be gone a few days?" Logan leaned against the porch railing, his fingers flexing around the top rail. The day he'd both waited for and regretted would come, may have arrived on the day he'd all but declared his love to Rose. If these were the Kennedy cattle rustlers, he was one step closer to taking his family back to big city life. He'd always known he wouldn't be safe living in Dodge once his cover was broken. Hell, none of them would be safe as far as he was concerned.

Pinkerton agents in this part of the country weren't

favorably looked upon among the roughnecks running rampant. Especially not one trying to blend in with the locals and pretending to be something he's not.

"I reckon so," Hawkins nodded, then jogged down the steps and remounted his black gelding. "We'll be waiting out back for ya. Saddle the bay for you?"

"Yes, best horse I've got for traveling for hours in the saddle." Logan watched Hawkins and his men round the corner of the house to the barn. Damn, this was the last thing he'd wanted right after marrying Rose. At least Lilly would have someone to look after her, should he not make it back alive.

He looked at the fear edged in Rose's eyes, his heart crushing.

"Logan, what did the Deputy Marshall and those men want?"

Panic streaked through the air between them. Logan closed the door, then took her in his arms. If this was his last moment with Rose, he wanted to feel her next to him.

Logan reached for his gun belt, strapping it around his hip. His heart ached at the fear in Rose's eyes, but this was his job. It was the reason he'd come to Dodge City. He did the only thing he could, he turned away stuffing a few items into a pouch.

"Pinkerton business." Was all he said. The less Rose knew the safer she and Lilly would be. He walked out the back door and across the yard to the barn, leaving his heart, his fear, and his love behind.

ROSE STOOD AT the back door watching Logan ride

away with Deputy Marshal Hawkins and several other men. A man, her husband, strapping on a six-shooter meant only one thing—trouble. Her heart filled rapidly with fear as the dust billowed in the wake of their southwest path. Letting the back screen door slam shut, she ran through the house and out the front door.

"Logan!" She yelled at the top of her lungs, bolting down the steps and across the barren yard. "Logan!" Rose kept running with her skirt hiked up almost to her knees. Dust splattered under her footfalls. She had to reach him. To tell him, someway, how she felt about him. What he meant to her.

"Whoa!" Logan pulled up the bay then slid out of the saddle. Handing the reins off to Hawkins, he broke into a run toward her. When he slowed she sprung into his arms. Her lips met his with a hunger she'd never experienced before. A hunger she couldn't define and only Logan could fulfill.

"Logan Granger, you'd better come back home in one piece riding upright on the back of that nag of yours." Rose let the tears filling her eyes spill down her cheeks, her insides quivering with both fear and elation. "If you're in a pine box you'll have a heap of explaining to do."

"Rose, my sweet Rose." Logan crushed her to him, kissing her long and hard as if his life depended on that single kiss. He held on to her, squeezing her as he spoke into her hair. "The horse and buggy are ready for you to drive into town. Lilly is at Etta May's waiting for us. Fetch her, then get what you need from Collar's to tide you over until I get back." He looked at her through

THE RELUCTANT BRIDE
(Brides Along the Chisholm Trail)

narrow eyes. Rose shivered when he leaned away, leaving a cold empty space. "You do know how to drive a horse and buckboard, don't you?"

Rose nodded her head even though her mind screamed no. She should be telling him that he was leaving man's work to her. That she considered driving that buggy into town to get Lilly and for them all to shop at Collar's was his job—not hers. But she didn't.

Her dark thoughts kept going back to Logan. To his coming back home for her and Lilly only to bury him in the ground. She couldn't think about needing to go into town to bring Lilly home. Or that she'd have to go through the pantry and make sure they had everything they'd need until Logan came back. Rose only wanted, needed, to think of and pray for, his safe return.

"I'll be home in a day or two around supper time, so have the table set and my favorite apple pudding waiting for me." When he released her completely Rose peered into his eyes through her tears. A new kind of sorrow glimmered near the surface, one that scared her, but she wouldn't let him know it.

She wouldn't allow him to ride away thinking, she wasn't capable of taking care of Lilly while he was checking on possible rustlers. She'd much rather he was off to rustle up drinks behind the bar at the Lady Gay, then chasing down cattle rustlers in the middle of nowhere.

If she had to be brave for all them, she would. If she had to fall to her knees and ask the Lord to take her and not him, she would. Rose would do whatever it took for Logan to return home in the same condition he rode out in.

"I will." Rose promised, then stepped away, releasing him from their bond. "Lilly and I will be waiting."

He walked back to the bay and with reins in hand mounted easily. He looked over his shoulder at her, the smile on his face wide and filled with something darn near to love. He tipped his hat and spurred the bay into a canter in order to catch up to the others.

Rose stood in the dust for several moments as the dirt settled around the hem of her dress until she could no longer see Logan. Wiping stray strands of hair back into place, she turned and shuffled back to the house mulling things over in her head.

Rose plopped down into the porch rocking chair, her gaze focused on the path Logan and the riders had taken. If she could sit here until the thunder of horses' hooves with Logan in the lead signaled his return, she would. She swiped at the tears running down her face.

Why hadn't she told him her secret? The reason Abigail Johnson hadn't arrived on the train several days ago. Because she couldn't let him go with any doubt on her credibility to look after his daughter. Because she didn't want Logan to rescind the new marriage agreement. Because she had deep feelings for him.

Rose guessed she'd fallen for Logan at some measure the moment she'd seen him waiting for her on the train platform. He'd looked as scared as she'd felt. There'd been no time for a proper introduction before he'd whisked her off to the preacher.

The old wooden rocker squeaked as it moved back

THE RELUCTANT BRIDE
(Brides Along the Chisholm Trail)

and forth. Rose took a deep breath, mustering up any courage she had to spare. She prayed for strength to get them through the next several days, and for Logan to come home safe and sound.

"A horse, the buggy, Lilly, and the back filled with goods for the pantry all depending on my non-existence skill at handling a hitched horse, let alone the buggy attached to said horse." Rose shook out the dust settled on her skirt, then walked through the front door to take inventory of the pantry.

She'd never driven a horse and buggy in her life!

CHAPTER SEVEN

THEY RODE STEADY, covering ground from Dodge to the Cimarron easily. The trail hot and dusty from a dry spring, Logan reined in next to Hawkins, then reached for his canteen.

"Do you have any notion where along the Cimarron they'd be hold up?" Logan took a swig of water, then offered the canteen to Gabe.

"Not exactly, just about twenty or thirty miles between them and us." Gabe waved off the offer of drink, then turned to his men. "We'll stop in a few miles, let the horses rest and grab some grub."

Logan nodded and with slight heel pressure urged the bay forward at a walk. "Old Simon say who gave this information so freely?"

"Said it was a stranger, someone new in town." Gabe's answer short and to the point, and highly unusual for him. Gabe Hawkins was a man of many words. So far this morning there hadn't been enough to fill a paragraph in a book.

Logan looked over at the deputy marshal who'd been a friend since Logan had arrived in Dodge City. Gabe's relaxed carefree banter gave way to visible tension in his shoulders and arms. His soft hands on the reins now clenched so tight one of Etta May's fresh eggs would have cracked spilling its yellow contents all over the saddle's swell. Not once since they'd left Rose and the homestead had his gaze met Logan's.

"Sam! You and Charlie ride on ahead see if there's a good place to rest the horses." Gabe rolled his shoulders, then shifted in the well broke in saddle. Whatever was on his mind, Logan hoped that he'd let it out before the sun set.

"Yes, sir! Come on Charlie," Sam called, riding past Logan at a canter.

Once the two deputies were out in front by a few yards, Logan turned to the deputy marshal. "Something you wanna talk to me about, Gabe?"

"How's married life treatin' ya? Are you happy with Rose?" Gabe kept his gaze straight ahead, his speech rushed. "Do you love her?" Gabe put down the reins then removed his hat, running a hand through his hair.

"Right fine, I reckon." Logan answered, swatting a fly pestering the bay's neck. "Is wantin' to know about what I've been doin' the past few days the reason you sent them boys ahead? Or are you just trying to see if married life would be in your future?"

Gabe settled his hat on his head, keeping his gaze on the horizon. Logan knew there was something he wasn't saying. "Whatever the hell is on your mind spit it out, so we can get on with catching those cattle thieves."

"How well do you know Rose?" Gabe's eyes were hidden under the brim of his hat.

"In just three days?" Logan's laughter fell on deaf ears.

Gabe asked the question again, this time with the tone of a lawman, not a friend. He looked Logan square on, "I asked you a question Logan Granger. How well do you know Rose?"

"She's kind hearted, handled Montana Sue quite well the other day. Sets a fair table at supper. Looks after Lilly right fine."

"This came this morning." Gabe pulled a folded piece of paper from his vest pocket, then handed it over to Logan. "One more thing, Montana Sue happened to be passing the telegraph office after leaving Etta May's. Judging from the smirk on her face when she brought it to me, I reckon she's read it."

The bay halted from the slight pressure on the reins. Logan set his seat and unfolded the paper. He read, then re-read the handwritten words from Mr. Pinkerton. Words instructing Gabe to put one Roseanne Duncan into protective custody, if she happened to be in Dodge City. There was a possible wrongful death where she worked back in Wisconsin. A key witness turned up missing and may be on the run. According to a reliable source, Logan's boss believed that a woman going by the name of Abigail Johnson was that witness. Gabe was supposed to protect the woman at all costs until things were settled regarding the incident. Mr. Pinkerton indicated he'd send an update when he had one.

THE RELUCTANT BRIDE
(Brides Along the Chisholm Trail)

"Thought you should know about it. There's a storm brewing with no rain in sight." Gabe nodded, urging his horse into a walk.

Logan opened and closed his mouth. He had no words. His fingers clenched the reins and the bay crow-hopped under the sudden pressure. Was Rose a runaway witness? Why didn't she tell him last night when he'd been spilling his guts out? Or even this morning when he'd suggested changing the conditions of their marriage contract? He'd thought all the lies were out in the open, evidently not.

"I have to go back to the house, Gabe," Logan called out, staring straight into the sun. His heart pounded in his chest with fear. Fear that he may lose the woman who held him in the palm of her hand. "Rose has a right to tell her side of the story. She's a witness not a murderer for heaven's sake. She has her reasons for running away, and I'll bet money it's a damn good one. She's not the type to commit a crime, I know that."

"She does and she will, but not until tomorrow. Johnny Barker will look after her until we get back. I spoke with Etta May, she's prepared a room for both Rose and Lilly to stay in until we get back." Gabe looked over at Logan, his eyes reflecting the same concern that ran through him. "If there's someone on her trail, she'd be better off in town, close to people who can protect her."

"She'll probably refuse." Logan smiled, a small surge of pride for his foolish wife. "Rose won't take kindly being watched over like a child by Etta May or Johnny. I'm not sayin' she wouldn't be grateful for the gesture, just not happy about it."

"That's what I figured. Johnny will be keeping an eye on your family without being obvious until you ride in." Gabe spurred his horse and rode to catch up to Sam and Charlie.

Logan's mind spun as he watched the deputy marshal ride off. Gabe was right, they had rustlers to check on, maybe bring in along with any cattle they might find.

Rose wasn't in harm's way, yet. The telegraph didn't indicate she was in immediate danger—not from the law in Wisconsin. No, the only danger she was in would be from Logan.

Once he got back, Mrs. Rose Granger had a lot of explaining to do.

#

ROSE STOOD NEXT to the horse hitched to the buckboard, hands on her hips. "I hope you know what you're doin' big guy, because I certainly don't."

Hiking her skirt up, she stepped up into the wagon. Taking the reins in hand, she settled down onto the seat every nerve in her body on fire. One ear of the horse cocked back at her, waiting for a command from her trembling fingers.

"Get me to town and back, and you'll have a big juicy apple added to your grain tonight." Rose clucked the way she'd heard Logan do, then gave the reins a quick jerk. The sorrel turned its head, looking at her with a big soft dark eye.

"I promise, really I do." Rose sucked in a breath, clucked once more, then gave the reins a harder snap this

THE RELUCTANT BRIDE
(Brides Along the Chisholm Trail)

time.

The sorrel stepped out, the buckboard lurched forward, jostling Rose sideways. Shaking in her boots, Rose quickly righted herself and drew in another deep breath releasing it slow and easy. "Well, that wasn't so difficult after all."

Rose bounced slightly on the seat of the buckboard; dust rose up around the horse's legs with each footfall. The wooden wheels creaked a sad and sorrowful tune that matched her mood.

"I should have been truthful with Logan before he rode out this morning with Deputy Marshal Hawkins. He has every right to know he married a deceitful woman before the new marriage contract is drawn up."

Rose kept her eyes straight ahead. Lost in thought she relied on the horse to know the way into Dodge City. She hadn't paid much attention when Logan was driving, she was too busy watching him. Admiring the way he handled the team of horses. The way his muscles flexed under rolled up sleeves. The way he made her feel inside the secret place every woman has. Over the past few days she'd unexpectedly come to care for both Logan and Lilly.

She hadn't meant to, but she had. And now Logan had ridden off into possible danger not knowing who she really was. Rose wasn't Abigail Johnson, matronly woman who only agreed to take care of his household and Lilly because she wanted adventure in her life.

She wanted to be Roseanne Granger, a woman who truly yearned to feel Logan next to her at night. To do all the things a wife and husband do when the house is still and quiet.

Instead she was Roseanne Duncan, a woman running from a man she'd seen kill his wife. Running from a man who had the ability to ruin her. Rose was the coward who couldn't stand up for a woman sent to the grave far too early in her life.

Logan didn't know that his wife, unlawful at that, was probably being hunted by the authorities. He didn't know his marriage was made of deceit.

Yet, hadn't she allowed it to happen with her lies the moment she'd accepted Abby's proposal?

The sound of a rider snapped her out of her thoughts. Rose focused on the figure coming out of a cloud of dust. One of Gabe's deputies appeared, slowing his black and white horse to a walk. Johnny Barker reined in alongside the buckboard, tipping his hat.

"Mrs. Granger, I was thinking since the deputy marshal and your husband are out chasing rustlers, you might need a hand."

Rose smiled, shading her eyes from the late morning sun. "Deputy Barker, I'd be pleased to have your company into town if that's what you're offering."

"Yes ma'am. I'd be right obliged to put up that gelding and buckboard for yer also, if you don't mind." Johnny offered, staying close to her. Rose guessed him to be about twenty-five or so, with dark hair dusting his collar. There was a gentleness about his face that soothed her.

They rode in peaceful silence for the next mile. Dodge City rose up ahead, the outline of the buildings visible through the sun. The livery stood off to the west

THE RELUCTANT BRIDE
(Brides Along the Chisholm Trail)

of town; she looked over at Johnny.

"You're doing right fine Mrs. Granger. Right fine for a city lady." Johnny beamed at her and the tension of the morning lessened. "Rein him to the left and then straight to Wilsons. I'll put him up until you and Miss Lilly are ready to return home. I'll be at the sheriff's office doin' paperwork."

Rose nodded, doing as he instructed she rounded the corner, heading straight for Wilsons. "Whoa." The command was soft and calm. Rose pulled the wagon to a stop, then tied the reins off and allowed Johnny to give her a hand down.

"Thank you. I hope you'll come by for supper tonight, Johnny Barker." Rose smiled, then turned toward the center of town.

Rose strolled over to Etta May's. Her heart felt a bit lighter knowing she'd be picking up Lilly. They'd shop for the items on the list Rose had written up, go back to Etta May's for ice cream before heading back home for chores and supper. Just because Logan was gone didn't mean she could ignore the chores, besides she'd promised the sorrel an apple.

She walked through the door of the eatery expecting to find Etta May and Lilly. Instead Montana Sue sat at a table in the corner, drumming her painted fingers on the polished wood.

"Where's Lilly?" Rose asked looking around the restaurant, her stomach rolling in anticipation. She didn't like Montana Sue being here waiting for her like a hawk waiting for its next meal. It meant she intended to interfere, or at least try to.

"You took your time gettin' here seein' Gabe left hours ago. I figured he'd return with you and Logan behind him. Guess I was wrong." Montana Sue snickered, her eyes filled with dark hatred. "She's in the kitchen with Etta May helpin' with tonight's supper."

Rose smiled as gratefully as she could to a queen bee in a hive. "Thank you, I'll go collect her now."

Montana Sue stood, her hands on her hips and skirts rustling along the floorboards as she came toward Rose. "Do you really think that's best for poor Lilly, you bein' a fugitive and all?"

Rose froze. Her legs unable to carry her to the kitchen where Lilly waited. "I haven't the slightest idea what you think you may know Montana Sue, but I can tell you it's not what you think."

Montana Sue laughed, then glared at Rose. "No? Well the way I see it you've married a man under false pretenses. Gone into his home. Moseyed on up to him and that sweet little girl of his, all the while the two of them thinking you're an angel from above." Montana Sue snorted then crossed her arms, staring icily at Rose. "We both know that's a lie, don't we *Roseanne Duncan*?"

Fingers sprayed across her breastbone, Rose swallowed the hard lump in her throat. She took several steps forward until she was inches from Montana Sue. "You don't have any proof of anything. If you did, you'd know the truth." Rose spun on her heel fisted hands at her side, then she stopped after a few steps. Looking over her shoulder she met Montana Sue's cold glare head on. "You'll never have Logan for your own, he doesn't love you in that way. You are his friend, nothing more. This is your last warning. Leave me and my family alone!"

"Or what? You'll kill me too?" Montana Sue stomped out the door her chest thrust out and her spine as rigid as a lightning rod. "We'll see about that *Mrs. Granger*!"

Rose released the breath lodged in her lungs and sank down into the nearest chair. Pent up tears rolled down her cheeks. Exhausted from the encounter she put her head on the table sobbing.

"THERE, THERE, NOTHING'S that awful to warrant so many tears my dear." Etta May's soft, motherly cooing washed over Rose like a warm cozy blanket.

Rose scanned Etta May's kind, weathered face and in that moment realized how much she missed her mother. "Etta May, I've made such a mess of things." Rose scouted the room, fear striking through her sadness "Where's Lilly?"

"Not to worry, she's up in the room I prepared for the two of you. I suspect she's sound asleep after working in the kitchen all morning with me."

"Thank you," Rose whispered, sniffling back the urge to cry again, her body sagging with relief.

"Now, why don't I go get us some tea and a piece of the apple pie Lilly baked." Etta May dashed into the kitchen, returning with the teapot, two cups and saucers, and two plates of warm pie.

"I've ruined everything for Logan and Lilly." Rose pushed the pie around on her plate. The fork slipped from her limp fingers, clattering onto the plate. Her arms tucked to her sides, Rose slumped down in her chair. She'd not only destroyed Logan's life; she'd also managed to do the same for an innocent child's future.

"Doesn't do no good to suppose somethin' that may not be true, child," Etta May scolded.

"I haven't been truthful with Logan," Rose choked down the sour taste of deceit lingering inside her mouth. "And, and I need to be before—" *Before I cause Logan more disappointment and shame.*

"Before someone tells him your secret?" Etta May swiped at her tear-filled eyes.

Rose looked at Etta May a fluttering feeling deep in her belly. The pain reflecting on the kindly woman's face made Rose sick to her stomach. Etta May was disappointed in her as well.

"A telegram came for the marshal this morning. Gabe came over and asked if I'd look out for Lilly while he took Logan out on a cattle rustling lead to show him the telegram."

Rose gasped, her heart racing like a wild mustang. "Logan knows who I really am?"

"Yes, by now I reckon he does." Etta May poured more tea, her hand trembling slightly. "So do I, and I suspect Montana Sue does also seein' as how she delivered it. But I want to hear what happened that was so horrible to make a fine young lady like you run away. Will you tell me everything, Rose?"

"Yes." Rose sat back, drying the tears brimming her eyes. "Roseanne Duncan is my name. I worked in the house of a very powerful man as a housemaid. One morning I rose early and started down the servant's stairs to the kitchen when I heard arguing in the hall. I peeked out the door just as the mistress tumbled down the stairs and the master stood there smiling…"

Rose continued with how Mr. Griswold threatened her. How Abby had been the one to answer Logan's advertisement for a bride. That it was at Abby's insistence Rose come in her place in order to protect herself from Mr. Griswold. So Rose took the train ticket tucked inside the envelope with the letter and tintype of Logan, and boarded the train coming to Dodge City.

"I owe Abby my life, Etta May." Rose sniffed, dabbing her tired eyes. "Abby gave up a life with Logan and Lilly for me. She gave up her life's adventure to save my life."

Etta May covered Rose's hand with one of her own, "Dear Rose, I'm not sure I wouldn't have done the same in Abby's place. The Lord has a plan for all of us, including you, Rose. And that man loves you. I see it on his face every time he watches you. Logan will understand."

"But we aren't legally married," Rose all but sobbed, twisting the napkin in her hand. *Thankfully we haven't shared the same bed, it'll make parting a bit easier when the time comes.*

"That, child will be the easy part!" Etta May smiled, her eyes lighting up like a tree at Christmas.

"Momma?" Lilly's tiny voice came rushing down the stairs. "Montana Sue said you are a bad person. That Daddy will have you locked up in jail and sent away."

Lilly flew into Rose's outstretched arms, her salty

tears leaving speckles of moisture on the bodice of Rose's dress. "No one is locking me up, Lilly. Not ever. And don't be mad at Montana Sue, she's a little confused by her heart right now."

Rose gazed at Lilly, wiping tears from her daughter's cheeks. Her heart swelled with love and acceptance. Lilly called her momma! No matter what was ahead, Rose was not going to leave Logan and Lilly without a fight. "Now, we've got to get a few things and go home, okay?"

Lilly nodded her head, wrapping her arms around Rose. "I love you Momma."

"I love you too Lilly," Rose cast her eyes up and closed them in a moment of silent prayer of thanks. "Let's thank Miss Etta May for looking after you all morning, and for showing you how to make the delicious apple pie. Then we need to get home to do those chores. And don't let me forget an apple for Daddy's sorrel!"

CHAPTER EIGHT

AFTER EATING SOME grub and resting themselves as well as the horses for a few hours, Logan and Gabe along with Gabe's deputies, pushed on for several more miles through the heat and dust until they came across several head of the missing Kennedy cattle now bearing an altered Double K brand. With the rustlers nowhere in sight, Logan helped roundup the cattle and drove the small herd toward Dodge City.

From the dark clouds gathering and the bellowing of the cattle, Logan had a feeling in his bones a storm was on the way. If they didn't get the herd close to the stockyard at Dodge, they'd have to at the very least take some shelter in a gully before the height of the approaching storm. If not their efforts would be blown away by chasing down the scattered beasts. Logan for one couldn't take the time to round up the scared longhorn, he had things pressing on the home front needing his attention.

"Looks like we might be gettin' wet," Logan reined

in next to Gabe, his gaze cast on the curtain of rain falling to the southwest moving toward them.

"I've been keepin' an eye out as well. We'll keep moving slow and easy so as not to spook 'em for as long as we can. Keep a look out for a place to hunker down in," Gabe glanced to the coming storm then back over to Logan. His eyes filled with regret, he shook his head lips pressed together. "I'm sure sorry 'bout giving you the news the way I did. I didn't see no other way to get you out of there to think things over. To be sure on how you felt about Rose."

Logan rocked with the rhythm of the gelding, his gaze settled on the several head of cattle in front of him. "There's nothing to settle on. Rose is my wife, plain and simple. Whatever she's done, she'll answer for it. I know you're wondering if I'll be sending her back and the answer is…hell, I don't know. I need to get a telegram to Mr. Pinkerton, and get Rose's side of the situation before settling on a judgment of any kind. Damn it Gabe, I asked her if she'd be willing to change our marriage contract before you came riding up. Maybe this is why she agreed so quickly. The fool thing is—"

"You're in love with her." Gabe nodded, a smile streaking across his face. "For what it's worth, it sounds to me like she witnessed something she shouldn't have. That it scared her enough to send her running from it. The telegram said to protect, not lock her up."

"Maybe I am. Maybe I ain't." The sky rolled with dark clouds. Logan pulled up the collar of his shirt and settled his hat tighter on his head. "Our luck is about to run out. These cattle might likely scatter if we don't get

THE RELUCTANT BRIDE
(Brides Along the Chisholm Trail)

them penned up somewhere and soon." Logan pointed to the southwest sky as the clouds rapidly merged into black ugliness.

The sky had turned from gray too black in a matter of moments. Logan spurred the gelding in the side riding off to the head of the small herd. Gabe rode to the opposite point, while Sam and Charlie took control of the rear keeping the cattle boxed and moving at a steady pace.

Logan stood in the saddle scanning the parched land ahead. "Damn, there's got to be a place or we're in a heap of trouble." He kept surveying the land hoping the gully they'd taken the longhorn from might have a branch up here. "There!" Logan shouted, then pointed over to a ravine. Gabe nodded then called out to his men pointing the possible shelter out to Sam and Charlie. Whistling and snapping lariats encouraged the stock forward slightly to the east. The clouds burst open as the men drove the bawling dogies down into the ravine. They had little time to prepare what shelter they could while the storm passed.

"We don't have much time!" Logan shouted above the rain and wind. "Tie your ropes together and herd the cattle in, but not too tight. We can tie it off on that tree stump." Logan pointed to a tall, round, sturdy looking stump. A curtain of rain poured over the brim of his hat. He climbed up the slippery slope and wrapped the end of his rope around what was left of the tree, tying it off. Tossing the rest of his rope to Gabe, the quick-and-dirty fence began to take form as each rope end was knotted together. "Let's hope this holds 'em."

A bolt of lightning streaked across the sky. Thunder clapped like cannon fire shaking the ground. Both horses and cattle pranced nervously while Logan and the others worked to tie off a makeshift corral.

The wind picked up as the sky turned an intimidating shade of green. Logan pulled the saddle and bridle from his bay. Throwing a loose rope around his neck, he'd be able to let go and give the gelding free rein should the need arise. He wanted the faithful animal to have a chance to run should the storm turn from bad too worse.

"What in blazes are you doin' Logan? If that horse runs off, you'll be without one and walkin' back to Dodge!" Gabe shouted about the wind and rain, his face tense. "A cowboy without a horse is a death sentence out here."

"I'd rather be walkin' than having to shoot a dying animal." Logan bellowed through the roar of the wind. "Take shelter Gabe, those cattle won't go far if they break through."

"Let's hope not if we're less one mount!" Gabe and his men plastered themselves against the dirt wall next to Logan. Sheets of rain fell from the sky, stinging skin not hidden under the brims of their hats and clothing. Even then the sting of ice penetrated the cotton shirts.

Cattle bawled. Horses snorted. Rain continued to pelt them, collecting around their legs. The wind roared in like a steam train. Logan looked up from under the brim of his hat. A dark twisting devil passed over them, spewing rocks and dirt.

Please Lord, keep my family safe.

THE RELUCTANT BRIDE
(Brides Along the Chisholm Trail)

#

ROSE HELD A bag in one hand and Lilly's hand with the other. They dashed across the busy dusty street and up onto the sidewalk, the heels of their boots clip clopping on the wooden planks. "I hope Deputy Barker will be able to get that sorrel harnessed and hitched up to the wagon for us so we can go home. I don't have the first notion on how it's done, do you?"

Lilly looked up at Rose, her forehead wrinkling in thought. "No, Daddy never showed me. Said I was too little."

"One day you won't be. Then you'll be able to do most anything as long as your daddy says it's okay." Rose smiled down at her daughter, knowing that it wouldn't be that long before Lilly would be bringing some young man home for their approval. As they approached the sheriff's office, Rose slowed their pace a little. She stopped next to the wide open door listening to the argument going on inside.

"Deputy Barker, I <u>demand</u> you put <u>that</u> <u>woman</u> in jail right this instant!" Montana Sue barked so loudly it caused passing town people to take notice. "She's a liar and a cheat with no business of being—"

"Now Montana Sue you know I can't do that. Mrs. Granger hasn't broken any laws here in Dodge." Deputy Barker's voice was calm with a touch of annoyance edging it. "You need to get a hold of yourself and settle down. I've got my orders from Deputy Marshal Hawkins, and they don't involve puttin' Mrs. Granger in the jail house!"

"Momma?" Lilly looked up at Rose, her eyes filled

with fear. "I don't want you to go to jail!"

"It's okay, Lilly. Nobody is going to jail." Rose gripped the little hand a bit tighter, and smiled down at her daughter. "Deputy Barker will help us get the wagon hitched, and we'll be on our way home."

Rose stepped through the open door, head held high, and about as nervous as a mouse in a barn full of cats. "Afternoon Deputy Barker. Is your offer to help me get the sorrel hitched to the wagon still good? We'd like to be on our way home now."

Turning to Montana Sue, she mustered up the best friendly smile she could seeing as how this woman viewed Rose as her enemy. If the situation were reversed, well no use supposin'. "Montana Sue, how nice to see you again. Lilly and I have just finished our shopping. I'd ask you to join us for some iced tea, but we simply must be getting home. Another time then maybe?"

Brows furrowed, Montana Sue gave the room the once over. Her gaze paused for a moment on Lilly standing next to Rose before returning her full attention to Deputy Barker. "This woman, whoever she claims to be, has no right to be in charge of a sweet, innocent child. She's wanted in another state by the law!"

"My momma ain't wanted by the law!" Lilly burst clinging to Rose's skirt, her eyes wide with fear.

"She isn't your momma, Lilly. She married your daddy to run away from trouble." Montana Sue knelt down, her arms stretched out. "Come to me and I'll keep you safe until your daddy comes home."

"No!" Lilly hid behind Lilly's dress, her tiny body

trembling. "I don't want to. You're a mean person."

"See what she's done to that poor child. She'd not only turned Logan against me, now she's done the same with Lilly. She's a con artist, deputy who should be locked up!" Montana Sue stomped her foot, her face red with rage.

"Montana Sue, if you don't stop your hollerin', it'll be you in this cell for the night." Deputy Barker threatened opening the nearest cell door, the keys dangling from his fingers.

"Well, I never!" Montana Sue turned and marched out of the sheriff's office, her skirts swishing along with her hips.

The deputy stood shaking his head. Montana Sue continued her determined step down the street toward the Lady Gay. "I'll never understand that woman." The deputy grabbed his hat and closed the cell door. "Let's get that wagon ready for you Mrs. Granger before those dark clouds movin' in burst wide open. Lord knows we sure could use the rain."

Deputy Barker escorted Rose and Lilly home at a hurried clip, then put up the sorrel and wagon for the night. After putting up the provisions in the pantry, Rose meandered to the barn with the promised apple in one hand and a pie in the other. Lilly skipped ahead anxious to see if there were any new kittens to play with.

"Thank you, Deputy Barker." Rose handed him the pie, then plunked the juicy red fruit into the sorrel's grain. "See I do keep my promises. Deputy, you've been a big help to Lilly and I today. I'm truly grateful for your generosity. What you've done for me today, well I don't know how to thank you."

"Montana Sue don't mean no harm, ma'am. She's used to Logan's attention due to Lilly is all." Johnny shuffled his feet a bit, nervously fingering the brim of his hat. "Well, dog gone it, she just don't know where the right place to look is all."

"Why Deputy Johnny Barker, are you sayin' you're in love with the hell cat?" Rose teased, sure that her eyes hadn't deceived her. Johnny Barker seemed smitten with one Montana Sue of the Lady Gay. Rose wished him luck roping that wild filly.

A blush of red crept up Johnny's neck as he put his hat on. "I best be gettin' back. Ain't right leaving the office and town open to rowdy cattle drovers." The deputy mounted his horse, nodded, and rode off at a canter back to town.

"Well, I'll be," Rose laughed out loud as the sky burst with a boom of thunder, shaking the ground beneath her feet. She looked up watching the dark clouds in the sky begin to twist and turn.

"Lilly, hurry we need to get to the house," she called out, closing the barn doors after Lilly ran out with a small gray kitten in her arms. "Take my hand and run with me as fast as you can. We need to get inside before the storm hits. Is there a root cellar, Lilly?"

"No Momma, Daddy said we didn't need no root cellar." Lilly cried out, her fingers wrapped tightly around Rose's hand. "Is a 'nado comin'?"

"I don't know." The wind picked up and roared. The rain falling in sheets felt like a thousand needles through her clothing. Rose picked Lilly up in her arms and ran up the back steps. Dropping Lilly inside the door, Rose pulled on the back door with all her strength as a black swirling cloud skipped across the horizon.

#

LOGAN RODE INTO Dodge beside the nervous longhorns pushing them into the stockyard holding pen. The once parched streets were now a sea of mud and debris. Logan and the others had kept in back of the storm once it passed over. They watched the destruction the twister left in its path as it hopped across the plains.

They all knew how lucky they'd been. The livestock hadn't scattered. The worst of the storm had blown right over them, dumping sheets of rain and hail stones into the gully. The massive twister retreated into the clouds for several minutes, leaving them in the falling rain.

Soaked to the bone, Logan's clothes were plastered to his body like a second skin. He craved a hot bath to chase the chill away, but not before he made sure his family was safe.

Family—did he really have one? Or would he lose Rose before they'd truly became man and wife in the biblical sense? Logan wanted more than a piece of paper between them. He wanted a life filled with love. And honesty, something they both needed to work on if they'd have a life together.

Logan led the drenched bay over to Wilson's Livery. With both horses available to pull the wagon he'd be more than happy to get his wife and daughter to the warmth and safety of their home. Once Lilly was snug in bed, he and Rose would settle in front of the fire.

He wanted her to explain the telegram to him and its meaning. Whatever, or whomever was after her, Logan needed to prepare himself to handle what came.

Guiding the horse through the door, Logan halted his heart pounding against his chest. Where in the devil was his buckboard and sorrel gelding?

"Wilson!" Logan called out, his legs stalled at the entrance of the livery.

"Here, in the back."

Logan marched to the rear of the barn. Wilson rubbed down a mare and her foal, talking in a soothing voice to calm them.

"Did Mrs. Granger come to town? I expected to see my wagon and horse here with the storm that passed through."

Wilson patted the mare's neck then stepped out of the stall, closing the door behind him. "Yes sir, she was in town. Deputy Barker took her and Miss Lilly home not long before the twister flew over. Damnedest thing I've ever seen. It bounced right over the town and headed north, its tail dragging along like the Devil."

Logan's stomach hardened like a boulder. His family alone in the house with neither of them knowing where to go or what to do. He'd never shown Lilly the root cellar entrance in the pantry for fear she'd play there. Besides, they'd spent most of their time in town until Rose came into their lives. There'd been no time to show Rose the trap door either. With the stronghold of the spring drought it never occurred to him they may need it.

Logan swung back up onto the wet leather of the

saddle then turned his horse toward the sheriff's office at a trot.

"Logan!" Montana Sue dashed from the wooden walk out onto the street in front of him, causing Logan to rein in the gelding quickly or run her down.

"Damn fool woman, what the hell are you doing?" Logan spat, keeping his temper checked.

Montana Sue stood next to him, her hand on his thigh. A muscle flinched at the sensation of her unwanted touch. "Praise the Lord, you're safe. I was so scared—"

"I don't have time for this." Logan jerked his knee, forcing her to relinquish her hold, then urged his mount forward.

Halting the bay in front of the sheriff's office, Logan called out, "Gabe! Johnny!"

Both ran out the door, drawing up at the hitching post.

"Can you ride out to my place? Rose and Lilly are there alone." Logan didn't wait for an answer. He turned his mount's head toward home, then spurred the animal in the side urging the worn out gelding into a canter until they reached the edge of town.

Logan rode hard until he saw what was left of his two story Lyman Bridges catalog house. His heart sank. The roof and part of the second floor were missing, lumber and furniture littered the yard. Jumping from the saddle, Logan took the porch steps at once then ran through what was left of the front door.

"Rose! Lilly!" he yelled his voice breaking in fear. They had to be here, alive. He couldn't live without them. He tore through the silent wreckage searching each room, stepping over items tossed around or torn from the walls. The staircase lay twisted against the library door. The settee Katie had bought just after they'd been married was turned upside down and teetered through a broken picture window in the living room.

"Lilly!" Logan pushed his way into the kitchen having found no trace of either Lilly or Rose in the front of the house. "Rose!" he screamed.

The back door hung on its hinges and the screen door was missing. Logan shoved the table and chairs from in front of the pantry. Every item from the shelves lay scattered across the floor. The cabinets were toppled over. A section of the back pantry wall sprawled over the door to the root cellar. His muscles sore and cramped from being in the saddle for hours on end, Logan fought back the nausea settling in his stomach.

Where in the world would they have gone? The barn? He stepped over the debris in the kitchen carefully.

"Mew"

He halted, cocking his head toward the sound.

"Mew"

There it was again. A kitten! If there was a kitten, then Lilly could be nearby.

"Lilly!" Logan cried out again tears of hope surfacing in his eyes.

"Daddy!" The cry soft and muffled edged with fear. His heart beat the speed of a wild Mustang on the run.

"Where are you?" Logan called out, keeping his fear at bay.

THE RELUCTANT BRIDE
(Brides Along the Chisholm Trail)

"Under the house," Lilly cried, her voice faint and weak. "Daddy, I'm scared."

"I know, honey. I'll get you out. Hold on." Logan worked feverishly picking up discarded provisions, tossing them into the kitchen. The hell with being careful and neat, his house could be replaced. His daughter never could.

"Logan?" Gabe called from the front of the house.

"In here!" Logan called back not once ceasing to get to his daughter. "Watch your step!"

Gabe came through the door his face ashen, dismay settling in his eyes.

"Lilly's down in the root cellar. Help me move these boards." Logan commanded, lifting a piece at a time. Blood raced through his veins hot and steamy. "I'm coming, Lilly."

"Daddy, I think Momma's hurt. She's not moving," Lilly's voice echoed the dread searing through Logan.

"Can you see Rose, Lilly?"

"Yes Daddy, she's on top of me. I can't move." Lilly's fearful cries reached Logan and his heart stopped. "Is Momma going to Heaven, Daddy?"

Rose couldn't be dead. He couldn't bear to lose another woman he loved so soon. He had plans for them all. A brother and sister or two for Lilly. Returning to his house in Chicago. To marry Rose properly.

Never one to lie to his daughter, Logan prayed he wasn't now. "No honey, she's sleeping. I'm sure she's fine."

Logan and Gabe hefted the last beam off the trap door. Logan yanked it open and slipped into the darkness. The ground damp from the storm, the muck squished under his boots.

"Gabe, hand me a lantern." Reaching up, Logan pulled the soft light into the dank space and his breath left his body.

In the corner he saw the matted brown hair of his daughter, a kitten next to her, and her entire body blanketed by Rose.

CHAPTER NINE

"LOGAN, YOU MUST eat something." Etta May's soft touch upon his shoulder did little to divert his vigil. "You'll do no good to Rose, or Lilly, if you don't keep your strength."

Logan heard the click of the tray set upon the table next to him. It had been twenty-four hours since he and Gabe had dug both Rose and Lilly out from under the damage left behind by the twister. For all of those twenty-four hours, each minute, each second that went by, Logan prayed for Rose to come back to them.

Doc Elliott said she'd be fine. That she sustained only minor bumps and bruises. What she needed more than anything was rest. When she woke, someone would send for him. Logan didn't give a darn what the doctor said, he wasn't leaving Rose's side.

Lilly appeared to have recovered far better than Rose. Etta May reported his daughter was nearly back to her usual six-year-old self. Etta May took over looking after her while he'd kept watch on Rose. He'd barely heard Montana Sue's ranting earlier when she'd faced off with Etta May about Lilly. Etta had all but kicked her out of her establishment.

Logan tried to spoon some of the soup into Rose's mouth with little success. The water from a moist rag, squeezed into the corners of her rose pink mouth, the only liquid he'd been able to get into her; and it wasn't much. He'd watched Katie disappear from his life, he'd not allow Rose to do the same.

"Rose, come back to us. Lilly needs you. She needs her momma to guide her, to play with her, to scold her—to love her." Logan took her hand, caressing the top of it with the pad of his thumb his heart aching. "It doesn't matter what happened before you came here. All that matters is that you stay with us. With me. I need you Rose, more than I could have imagined in so short of a time. I'll protect you until the day I die."

Bringing her hand to his lips, he softly kissed the center of her palm. "I love you, Roseanne Duncan, with all my heart," he barely whispered against the sensitive spot.

"Logan?" Rose moaned, the gray parlor of her cheeks slowing returning to a faint pink hew.

"Rose!" Logan gushed, unshed tears flowing over his cheeks. He didn't care if it was manly or not. He didn't care who did or didn't see him cry. Rose had come back to him. "You had me scared to death!"

Rose licked her lips, her eye lashes fluttering. "Is Lilly—" She began, then coughed dryly. "I'm so thirsty," she complained, the tip of her tongue skimming her parched lips.

"Lilly is fine and will be happy to know her momma's awake." Logan held her hand tighter, not willing to let her go. "Here, have a sip of soup. Etta May brought it in a short time ago." Logan dipped the spoon, filling it. Lifting her head with one hand, he brought the spoonful of the golden chicken soup slowly to her lips with his other hand.

Rose swallowed then closed her eyes for a moment, drawing in a shaky breath. "Logan, I have to tell you—"

"I know, Rose," Logan began, dipping the spoon into the bowl scooping more of the soup.

"No, you don't." Rose opened her eyes, tears brimming along the edges of her long lashes. "My name is Roseanne Duncan, not Abigail Johnson. I have no right to be mother to Lilly or wife to you. In fact—"

"Rose—"

"Please Logan, let me finish what I have to say." Rose's eyes pleaded with him, and he nodded for her to continue. Logan shuffled his chair closer to the bed, placing his free hand on her heart. They'd go through the story together joined by their flesh, hearts, and soul. Logan knew together they'd be able to get through anything. Good. Bad. Ugly. As long as they were all together—as a family.

"Logan, I've never been so scared of someone before. I worked for the Griswold's for several years. Granted, they may not have been the ideal family, but Mrs. Griswold always showed me kindness. But that morning, when Mrs. Griswold lay at the bottom of the stairs." Rose continued to tell her side of what the Pinkerton telegram meant. Logan squeezed her hand in anger as she described the threat her former employer, Atticus Griswold, bestowed upon her the morning she'd witnessed the "accident." Her small, gentle hand trembled in his as she spoke of the fear of what Griswold insinuated he could do to her. How her friend Abby had given up her chance of "an adventure" by sending Rose in her place to marry Logan in name only, and become a mother figure to Lilly.

She ended with how she'd found the trap door, had shoved Lilly down into it, and covered the child with her own body to protect her.

Tears flowing down both their cheeks, Logan pulled Rose into his arms and they cried together. Cried out of sorrow for a senseless death. Cried for what Abby gave up to protect her friend. Cried for having survived what life—good and bad—had dealt them. Their tears saying more than words could ever express.

"Logan?" Gabe's voice filtered through Logan's grief. He wiped his face before turning to face the deputy marshal.

Logan knew what was coming. Gabe would have no choice but to do his duty as deputy marshal. Logan couldn't fault him for it, but he sure as hell would fight him every inch of the way—right or wrong.

"Hi, Deputy Marshal Hawkins," Rose greeted, her soft voice still weary from the ordeal.

"Mrs. Granger, it's good to see you are finally awake. Now maybe this nitwit will eat something." The smile on Gabe's face didn't reach his eyes. A rock slammed to the bottom of Logan's stomach. He wasn't going to like the reason for Gabe's visit or what he had

THE RELUCTANT BRIDE
(Brides Along the Chisholm Trail)

to say.

"This isn't easy for me to say to either of you with all that's happened." Gabe fiddled with the brim of his hat, his eyes darting between them. "Until I can be sure of Rose's safety, I want to put her in protective custody—at the jail."

Logan sprung to his feet. "No way in hell is that going to happen!"

#

"BE REASONABLE, LOGAN. And before you say a word, I know you have some qualifications. I'd rather not take the chance of getting you involved or killed. It's my job to handle Rose's safety, not yours at this point." Gabe stood firm behind his desk, his authoritative stance far from threatening to Logan. "Until I receive further word, Rose will need to stay here."

"Reasonable? You want me to be reasonable when all you want to do is throw my wife in a cell?" Logan slammed his fist down on the desk, papers scattering onto the floor. "She's not fully recovered, Gabe. Being in the cell will do her no good. It may hamper her full recovery. She needs to be home with Lilly and me, not in a cell."

"Deputy Marshal Hawkins, I *demand* you put that criminal in a cell right this instant! Rose Granger, or whatever she's calling herself, poses a danger to the law abiding citizens of Dodge City!" Montana Sue flounced through the door of the small office, nose in the air, the heel of her boots clicking loudly on the wooden floor.

Logan reached out, grabbing her by the arm, swinging her about until his face inches from hers. "If you think for one minute that you've got a snowball's chance in the desert with me, you are sadly mistaken, Montana Sue," Logan hissed, his face burning with rage. "I don't now, nor have I ever felt more than friendship toward you. Rose…is…my…wife!"

"That girl is no more your wife than, than…" Montana Sue stood in front of Logan, her hands planted firmly on her hips. "The woman is a con. She's married you under a false name, making the marriage a sham. It's not legal." She turned to Gabe, her eyes daring him to defy her. "It's *your* civic duty to toss her in a cell."

"She's right, Logan." Rose stood leaning against the door frame, her face awash with guilt. "I did deceive you, that's true. I married you under a false name, as well as false pretenses." Her eyes floated in a sea of tears, threatening to break shore any moment.

Logan stared at her in disbelief, his heart cracking into pieces. One thing was certain, Rose was not going to go anywhere without him. He loved her. He knew it in his heart and soul she loved him too. They didn't need words when their hearts spoke volumes.

"Fine, lock me up with her. Where she goes, I go." Logan crossed his arms, his posture stiff, daring Gabe to do it. To lock him up in a cell along with Rose. Logan said he would gladly go. He'd spend his days in that small space with her. Etta would look after Lilly, and stand fully behind his decision to join his wife in her hour of need. When his protest was over and Gabe released them both, they'd go home to salvage whatever was left of their home…and their marriage.

Rose hobbled over to a chair, sitting down slowly.

THE RELUCTANT BRIDE
(Brides Along the Chisholm Trail)

"Deputy Marshal Hawkins, may we have a few moments—alone?"

"Of course," Gabe grabbed his gun belt, strapping it around his hip. "Montana Sue, there's no place for you here. Go back to the Lady Gay," he ordered, taking a hold of her elbow and pushing her toward the door.

"Well!" Montana Sue stomped out of the office, her skirts billowing behind her.

Gabe followed in her wake, closing the door behind him.

"Rose, please." Logan knelt down next to her, his life ending before the words were spoken. "You're innocent of any crime. A victim of circumstance. I know how it sounds. Cliché at best." He swallowed the lump of fear in his throat. He'd sworn to protect her as his wife, and he was failing miserably. "I beg you, please don't do this so easily. There isn't a warrant, only a telegram asking, asking mind you, that Gabe put you under protective custody. It doesn't say to put you in jail."

Rose smiled, a hand gently caressing his cheek. "Logan, we both know the truth. Until Gabe receives word, he feels as deputy marshal that he has no recourse but to set me up here in a cell. He's only doing his duty the only way he knows how. And you need to do yours as Lilly's father. As much as this pains me, you need to find her a truthful woman who'll love her as I do. Marry and forget about me. The two of you have suffered enough without having my running from a situation cause any more pain." Rose sniffed, tears flowing down her cheeks. "Think of the impact this will have on Lilly."

Logan opened then closed his mouth. He was at a loss for words. His chest tightened. His heart was ready to explode. He covered her hand with his, her skin tingling against his palm. They were both afraid. Afraid of saying the truth of their unlawful union. He wouldn't have it!

"No, I'll never marry another ever again. Rose, you're my wife."

Rose let her hand fall onto her lap, her slender fingers intertwined with the skirt of her dress. "No, no I'm not Logan; not legally. We've been playing house like two children these past months. It's time to grow up and do what is right by Lilly, before we take it too far. Before—"

Rose stood slowly and drew in a deep breath. Logan's gaze followed as she shuffled into a cell, the door clanging shut behind her. "Go and leave me. I'm not the woman for you, and certainly not a respectable mother for Lilly. It would break my heart to bring shame upon your good name."

She turned her back on him. Every ounce of his life force flickered off and on.

"This isn't over, Rose. I'll get to the bottom of the accident, then we'll be free to live as man and wife." Logan vowed, stomping out of the marshal's office.

FROM THE CELL window, Rose watched as Logan bounded around Dodge like a man possessed. First the telegraph office, then over to Etta May's where he'd finally appeared with a saddlebag draped over his shoulder only to run across the street to the train depot.

THE RELUCTANT BRIDE
(Brides Along the Chisholm Trail)

Lilly was nowhere in sight. Rose prayed she was safe with Etta May, hopefully unaware of Rose being locked up, even if it was by her own insistence. She knew her situation would not stay hidden for long. Dodge City may be growing, but news still traveled at the speed of lightening. No secret worthy telling was safe.

The Atchison, Topeka & Santa Fe train whistled its arrival as it began its assent into town. Rose's breath hitched in her chest at the sight of Logan standing on the platform. The deputy marshal stood next to him as the two carried on in an animated conversation. Tears stung her eyes. Her heart ceased pumping life into her soul.

Logan was leaving town and there wasn't a thing she could do to stop him. The train that brought her to Dodge City in the spring roared slowly up to the platform. In a twist of fate, it would be the very train to take the only man she would ever love away. Tears rolled down her cheeks as the engine pulled away from the platform, her words never reaching the man they were meant for.

"I love you, Logan Granger."

LOGAN HAD ALL but run to the train depot for fear of missing his chance to board. After Rose had locked herself in one of the marshal's jail cells, he'd checked the train schedule and found one leaving for Kansas City would be arriving within an hour. He'd had enough time for a quick telegram to the Chicago Pinkerton office, telling his boss of his intentions. He'd gone to Etta May's asking her to watch Lilly, explaining he'd be back as soon as he could. While she'd packed him some jerky, biscuits, and salt pork, he sat Lilly down telling her that she might hear some awful lies about Rose. He explained how he was going to find the proof to clear her name. Lilly whimpered, then nodded her head, telling him she loved him and her momma. That she'd visit her each day until he returned. It broke his heart to leave his six-year-old with the task of letting Rose know how much she was loved, and needed. He held Lilly for a moment, then gathered his warring emotions. Etta May handed him the saddlebag filled with provisions, and he'd jogged over to the depot as the train whistle announced its arrival.

He'd stood on the platform, arguing with Gabe Hawkins as the train screeched to a stop. Gabe pleaded with him to stay. That Logan would do no good running off to Chicago, leaving his daughter and Rose behind. But Logan locked the words from his brain. He'd go to Chicago and find out what the hell had happened in the Griswold household that morning. He'd told Etta May he'd be back within a month to fetch Lilly.

He'd had to explain to his six-year-old daughter that he was leaving, but only long enough to make sure Rose was safe. Lilly had swiped her tears from her face, given him a kiss and whispered in his ear, "Save Momma, Daddy." It was all the encouragement he needed to dash any apprehension from his mind.

Being on this train going back to a place he'd thought he'd never return to may seem foolhardy to some, but Logan saw it as the only way to clear his wife's good name. He didn't care what happened to her

THE RELUCTANT BRIDE
(Brides Along the Chisholm Trail)

before she came west. He didn't give a damn what others thought of her. What mattered was how he cared for her. How his young daughter had warmed up to Rose enough to call her momma.

That he loved Rose Duncan with all his heart, and couldn't image their life with her in it.

The landscape between Dodge City and Kansas City was nothing more than a blurred painting. He'd forgotten how uninviting this land was in comparison to the lushness of Illinois. How lifeless Kansas seemed to him. Logan closed his eyes, remembering the day Rose had stepped off the train. How on that spring day in May, he'd been swept off his feet. Head over heels for a woman he hadn't expected.

Thinking back on that day now, Logan realized that he'd known in his heart Rose wasn't Abigail Johnson. His only thought was to marry the girl before she had time to change her mind.

Logan remembered the numerous late nights when the house was quiet, he'd stood at Rose's bedroom door watching her sleep. It had taken all his will power not to slip into bed next to her. For days he'd ached to hold her in his arms. To feel his lips upon hers, their hearts pounding fiercely in unison.

And then, when he'd finally found enough courage to change their marriage contract, all hell had broken loose. Now, here he was on a train back to Chicago, to find a way to keep the woman he loved in their lives.

"Next stop Kansas City!" The conductor announced walking through from car to car.

As the train pulled into the depot and slowed next to

the platform, Logan swung the saddlebag over his shoulder, glancing out the windows. People gathered waiting for loved ones, or to board the next train.

Making his way down the steps and through the crowd, he strolled along the platform, looking for his boarding window. Finding the right one, he stood in line waiting to hand over his ticket when a hand grabbed his arm. He turned and looked into the face of a kindly middle-aged woman.

"Excuse me, sir. You're Logan Granger, aren't you?"

CHAPTER TEN

LOGAN GAZED INTO the desperate eyes of the matronly woman before him. Nothing about her sparked an ounce of familiarity. Her clothing, while fashionable, was a few seasons older. Her hair streaked with shades of auburn and gray here and there, was unruly under a hat that had seen better days.

"Are you or are you not Logan Granger?" She demanded, her irritation at his delayed response noted by her pursed lips.

Logan drew his brows together, clearing his throat. "Yes ma'am. Do we know one another?" The muscles in his neck tensed, waiting for an opportunity to step away from the woman.

"Thank goodness! I thought I'd recognized you from the tintype you'd sent." Her words rushed forward on the breath she'd been holding. She closed her eyes muttering something or another, then graced him with a smile as wide as an eagle's wing span.

Logan searched his mind. Who would he have sent

a picture of his likeness to? Certainly not to this woman who could be his aunt. "I must apologize ma'am, I can't seem to make a connection between you and me."

"Ahh, well I can see you are confused. As you rightly should be." The woman placed her valise at her feet, extending a hand out to him. "My name is Abigail Johnson, the woman you had intended on marrying."

All of Logan's breath vacated his lungs. It felt like he'd been sucker punched in the gut. He stared dumbfounded at the woman offering her hand in greeting. His lungs filled with relief, and he grasped her hand in his, surprised by the firmness of her grip.

"You're Rose's friend, Abby?" Unable to keep relief out of his words, Logan fought the instinct to pick Abby up and twirl her around in a large circle of joy. While Miss Abigail Johnson was a becoming woman, Logan knew she had not been the woman for him. God had sent the woman meant to be his other half, Rose Duncan.

"Yes," Abigail smiled, her face lighting up at the mention of Rose.

"Rose never said you were coming. What are you doing here?" Logan couldn't imagine Rose didn't know her friend was coming for a visit. Surely she would have mentioned it to him. If nothing else, as she locked herself into one of Gabe's cells

"I needed to see Rose. She's been living a lie and—" Abigail stalled, lowering her lashes slightly.

"She's been on the run." Logan finished for her. "The truth reached us a few days ago. Rose told me her side of the truth, as the telegram only said she was wanted and needed protection. I'm on my way to Chicago to clear her."

Abigail smiled, her eyes sparkling. "You have fallen in love with her. I had hoped you would."

Logan felt the warmth of intimate knowledge sweep up the back of his neck. "Yes ma'am, with all my heart. My little girl, Lilly, does as well and has taken to calling her Momma."

"Then we need to have a conversation, Mr. Granger, and we need it now. I have a few items that Rose will be happy to see." Abigail patted her valise, turned and walked toward the depot restaurant.

"Miss Johnson, I don't mean to be rude, but why travel all the way from Wisconsin to Dodge City, when you easily could have either sent a telegram or had the items shipped along with a note?" Logan rubbed the back of his neck, looking down at his boots. "Surely nothing is so important that you'd need to travel all this way to deliver a message."

"Hmm, well yet here you are determined to travel all the way to Chicago, then north to Wisconsin, to do what your Pinkerton people could very well do. You feel it's important enough for you to do the investigation yourself, trusting no one else to the task." With a glimmer of amusement in her eyes, Abigail pointed out the obvious, then chose a table near the window and sat as Logan pulled out her chair. "Mr. Granger, if it'll ease your suspicion any, I have pressing matters in Dodge City. One of which is delivering what's in this envelope to Rose."

"What's in the envelope?" Logan took a seat across

the table from her. Miss Johnson's being here was either good news, or she harbored bad news regarding Rose being wanted as a witness to a possible murder.

"Tea, Miss Johnson?" Logan asked politely as the waitress waited to take their order.

Abigail laughed out loud, the sound rich and full. "No thank you. I'd much rather have a strong cup of coffee, black. Tea, in my opinion, is for the refined, and I am as far removed from that as is possible."

Logan chuckled, then ordered two cups of black coffee. "Now, what is it that Rose needs to know?"

Abigail sighed, pulling a package from her valise and setting it on the table. "First of all, let me ask you something. Is Rose happy, Mr. Granger? Really happy with her life in Dodge City?"

Logan thought for a moment, then smiled. "Yes, I believe so. At least up until the past few days she has been. We'd even talked of re-negotiating our marriage contract. Then the other day, I had to ride out with Deputy Marshal Hawkins to check on some cattle. It was then he gave me news that came about her being wanted. A tornado almost destroyed our home that same day, and things have gone downhill from there." Logan glanced over the brim of the steaming coffee, weighing his next words.

"She'd locked herself up in jail. Told me to leave her alone, and to find a respectable woman to marry and be a mother to Lilly. Which I have no intention of doing." Logan felt as if he were on trial and being drilled by an overprotective aunt.

"That certainly sounds like Rose. I'm willing to bet

her heart broke as she said those words. But she's stubborn and probably thinks she's protecting you."

"I know mine did. I made a rash decision to go to Chicago and plead with my boss to let me do my own investigation. If I don't find anything that clears her involvement, then I'll return to Dodge, pack up my family, and move farther west. I'll do anything to keep us together."

"And Rose?"

"Rose is a part of my family. Our family."

"And who is this boss you need to talk with? I thought you were a respectable man in Dodge City."

Logan sat back, toying with the cup. "I am, Miss Johnson, as an undercover bartender in Dodge at the Lady Gay. I'm a Pinkerton agent assigned to Dodge to find cattle rustlers for a wealthy Texas client."

Abigail's eyes widened, and she again laughed out loud. "Well then, Mr. Granger, you really need to rethink your plans."

She pushed the package in front of him then rose from her seat. Logan pulled out the letter sporting the Pinkerton Agency seal. His heart beat wildly. The words he read popped off the page.

Stunned, Logan shoved the paperwork back into the package and followed Miss Abigail Johnson out of the restaurant. All thoughts of catching the next train to Chicago forgotten.

#

"Momma?"

Rose looked up, joy filling her heart at the sight of Lilly. Just as quickly, sorrow burned it away.

"Lilly, what are you doing here? The jail is no place for a child." Rose's body defied her words as her arms automatically extended to the girl. She needed to feel her daughter next to her, as best she could through the bars.

"Oh, Momma!" Lilly flew into Rose's arms, plastering her body against the steel bars of the cell. Little whimpers muffled against Rose's dress.

"I thought she needed to see you." Etta May stood in the doorway, holding a covered basket in her hands. "Gabe, Deputy Marshal Hawkins, thought you might be hungry, so here we are."

Rose pushed on the door, surprised when it moved. "Will I be in trouble if I come out?"

Etta May chuckled. "No dear, you are free to move about the office. Gabe never locked the door, because you aren't a prisoner. You are under protective custody, not under arrest."

Rose pushed the door harder until it opened fully. She didn't recall it being this heavy when she'd marched in and closed it behind her after telling Logan to leave her. She soon realized, after several hours in the small square with a bed made of planks, she'd wished she'd thought the situation through before acting on impulse. Stepping through it, she felt like a song bird freed from its cage.

"Lilly, I'll take that hug all over again," Rose cried, anxious to wrap her arms completely around her daughter. This was so much harder than telling Logan to leave her. Logan was a grown man, whose common sense would eventually convince him she had done the right thing by pushing him away. Lilly, on the other hand, being a young girl, was not yet aware of the way of the world around her.

"Momma?"

"Yes, Lilly." Rose peered down onto the sweet angelic face, smoothing Lilly's ruffled hair with her hand.

"Daddy left on the train for Chicago. He said I have to be brave and not to listen to what people say about you." Lilly snuggled closer into Rose's embrace, her tiny heart thumping against Rose's tummy.

Tears stung Rose's eyes. She willed them back as she knelt down to look into Lilly's fearful eyes. "Well, your daddy is a very smart man. And you, my sweet daughter, a very, very brave girl."

Etta May cleared her throat drawing Rose's attention. "None of us is very smart if we let this fried chicken, potatoes, and gravy get cold. I ain't feedin' it to the dogs."

Rose hugged Lilly again, then dished up a plate for both of them as they all gathered around Gabe's desk to eat an early supper.

"He's coming back, Rose," Etta May said, putting a hand on her shoulder as she poured milk into the glasses. "He loves you, as much as he does Lilly."

Rose nodded, stirring her gravy and potatoes together, wondering if Etta May was right. She thought of the kiss she'd shared with Logan a few days ago, and her heart swelled. She did love him, there were no two ways about it. When it happened she couldn't imagine—only that it did. But did Logan love her the way she did him? She'd give up everything to protect Logan and

Lilly…including her freedom.

As they finished the early supper with talk of a book Lilly was reading, the train whistle sounded, signally its arrival into town.

"Duty calls. I've got to make sure there's plenty of coffee for those folks. I'll pick up these dishes as soon as the restaurant clears out." Etta May stood, wiping her hands over the ever present flour sack apron. "Come along, Lilly. You can read your momma that story book when we return."

Rose held Lilly for a moment, tears settling in the corner of her eyes once again. She gave the child a kiss on top of her head, then scooted her off with Etta May as the train squealed into town.

LOGAN STEPPED OFF the train feeling like it was the first time he'd arrived. With the court papers in his possession, Dodge City felt more like home than ever before. The question was, would Rose feel the same way?

"So this is the infamous Dodge City," Abigail remarked standing next to Logan. "Well it certainly is different than—"

"Daddy! Daddy you're home!"

Logan swung around just in time to catch his daughter as she sprung into his arms. He squeezed her tight, kissing her forehead.

"Lilly, I'd like you to meet Miss Abigail Johnson. She's—"

"Not gonna be my momma!" Lilly protested, her voice as threatening as a six-year-old could be. "I already have a momma; her name is Rose!" She scowled from Logan to Abigail.

"Lilly Marie Granger, you will apologize at once, young lady," Logan scolded, embarrassed his normally well behaved child had turned into a smart mouthed street urchin within a day.

"I'm sorry," Lilly said, her eyes down cast.

"Miss Lilly, I completely understand what you mean. You love your momma, don't you?" Abigail looked at Logan, her words clearly meant for him.

"Yes, ma'am," Lilly answered, her feet lighting on the wooden planks as Logan slowly lowered her to the ground.

"May I meet this wonderful momma who has filled your lives with so much love?"

Lilly's eyes lit up, then faded into sadness. "Daddy, would Momma want to meet this woman when she's in jail?"

"Shhhh, Lilly, or the whole town will hear you." Logan laughed, taking his daughter's hand. "I think that meeting Miss Johnson would be exactly what your momma would want, don't you, Miss Johnson?"

"Oh yes, yes indeed, Mr. Granger. Then I really must attend to my other business in town once I know that Rose is well taken care of." Abigail reached down for Lilly's hand, and Logan was surprised when his daughter took it. "Miss Lilly, would you take me over to see your momma...after a big chocolate sundae?"

Lilly looked up at Logan, her eyes as big as saucers. He nodded, and then watched as the two walked over to Etta May's. He drew in a deep breath, the envelope tucked under his arm. Abigail gave him the gift of breaking the good news to Rose himself, and he'd be forever thankful to her. Stepping off the depot platform, Logan began to walk across the street and down to the sheriff's office.

"Logan!" Gabe came trotting up next to him, his eyes hidden under his hat. "Who was that woman with you on the train? And what's in that envelope you've got there?"

"That woman is an angel sent to me from Wisconsin. Miss Abigail Johnson approached me at the Kansas City station. Evidently, she's traveled all the way to Dodge for two reasons. One to let Rose know she's not a witness to a murder anymore. And the second one she wouldn't elaborate on."

Gabe coughed, his hands loose around the horn of his saddle. "I received a telegram an hour after you left telling me the same thing. You should have stayed here, and not wasted your money getting on that train. Where's Lilly?"

"Over at Etta May's for ice cream with Miss Johnson. I'm on my way over to see Rose now."

"Hmm, well then. I'll give you some privacy and go check on…Lilly." Gabe gave his horse a soft kick and traveled over to Etta May's.

Logan walked over to the sheriff's office, feeling like a bridegroom on his wedding day. What if Rose decided she wanted to go back with Miss Johnson on the next train? Would he let her walk out of their lives without putting up a fight for the woman he loved? Saying a silent prayer for guidance, he walked into the jail.

"Rose?"

The woman he loved spun around, her hands full of dirty dishes. "Logan," she cried, dropping the plates onto the desk. "I didn't...I mean I thought..."

He scooped her up in his arms, showering her with kisses before she could utter one more word.

"Lilly told me..." Rose said when Logan released her.

"Told you what?"

"Well, over supper that she and Etta May brought, that you'd gone to Chicago. Did something happen to change your mind?"

He laughed, pulling her into him. "Yes, something did happen. But first I have a serious question for you, and I want an answer before I say one more thing."

"What more could be said, Logan? You need an honest woman in your life, not one that is wanted by the law," Rose argued, her words falling on deaf ears. "That situation hasn't changed. I'll not ruin your reputation insisting you honor our agreement. I'm not that kind of person."

"I have an honest woman in my life, the problem is, she doesn't seem to believe she's married to me. She's my wife, only not in the way I want her to be. Something I plan on changing." Logan got down on one knee, holding Rose's hand, afraid to let go. "Roseanne Duncan, will you give me the honor of becoming my wife? To have as many babies as the good Lord sees fit? To help me raise Lilly to become a beautiful young woman like you?"

"But Logan--" she began, tears rolling down her face.

"Just answer my questions, Rose." Logan's pulse was pounding in his wrist. Every nerve in his body on fire. "Please, Rose, would you become my wife—my legal wife and all that it entails?"

"Yes, Logan!" she cried, falling into his arms, knocking him over and onto the floor.

"Good, because Miss Roseanne Duncan, you are a free woman. And if that isn't enough of a surprise for you, I met a woman on the train in Kansas City who happened to be carrying these documents. They indicate your former employer, Mr. Atticus Griswold, admitted to pushing his wife down the steps and threatening you with all manners of ruination." His hands shaking, Logan passed her the envelope. Rose pulled each document out, and he reveled in the surprise on her face. The joy in her eyes said volumes.

"Abigail is here?"

"Yes, she's got Lilly over at Etta May's for a chocolate sundae. Gabe was headed that way to join them, leaving us completely on our own."

"Well, Mr. Granger, if you think for one moment you can have your way with me before we are legally wed, you are sadly mistaken. At least not before I get my ice cream sundae!"

EPILOGUE

"I CAN'T BELIEVE you're here, Abby, and that you answered a mail order bride letter yourself!" Rose continued to fuss with her hair, placing the daisies in just the right places. "Who is this man? Someone here in Dodge?"

"Let's not talk of that right now, Rose. It's your wedding day, not mine." Abby brushed the lace veil into place with her hand. "Really, Rose, you must quit fussing about it."

"Yes, but…"

"Hush now, child, it's time to make your appearance. Your family is waiting downstairs for you."

Rose looked at her friend's reflection in the mirror. Abby had given up her chance of an adventure to save her from what they believed to be a dangerous man. If it hadn't been for Abby recognizing Logan at the train station in Kansas City, Rose may not be standing here waiting to marry Logan Granger. She was about to be a married woman and a mother to a beautiful six-year-old girl all in a matter of moments. The thought filled her with joyful bliss.

The young woman in the white dress staring back at her was a far cry from the scared, and reluctant bride who'd stepped off the train in Dodge City several months ago. Rose had lived through a tornado, warded off a jealous woman, thrown herself in jail to protect the man and daughter she loved with all her heart.

The piano downstairs in the Dodge House parlor started playing the wedding march. Rose looked over to Abby, picked up her bouquet of daisies and sage brush, then walked to the top of the steps.

Everyone in town, including the once jealous Montana Sue, stood in various places throughout the parlor. Abby, serving as her maid of honor, now stood next to Deputy Marshal Gabe Hawkins. Gabe stood in as Logan's best man. Rose wondered at their relationship, and if Gabe had been the one to send for a bride of his own. Too busy with her own wedding, she'd never questioned them. She trusted God, and time, would take care of it, and Abby would finally find her adventure with a man to love and cherish her.

Rose's soon-to-be daughter, Lilly, stood next to her father, a matching bouquet in her hands. But it was Logan and Logan alone who had eyes for only her. She walked slowly down the steps. Her gaze focused on the man whom she trusted to give her all the love he could. She reached him, hooking her hand in the crux of his elbow, allowing him to lead her over to Preacher Samuels.

"Dearly beloved, we are…"

THE RELUCTANT BRIDE
(Brides Along the Chisholm Trail)

Logan brought her hand to his lips, gently kissing away the nervousness running through her. She smiled, anxiously waiting to say those two little words...I do.

THE END

BONUS EXCERPT

THE MARSHAL'S BRIDE
Brides Along the Chisholm Trail, Book 2

CHAPTER ONE

Dodge City
1877

"She's got to be there, Spade. Her telegram was quite clear." Marshal Gabe Hawkins sat on his black gelding at the corner of the jail, watching as the train steamed into Dodge City. The hot steel wheels hissed and screeched to a halt along the iron rails, causing sparks to fly in the air. The steam from the engine's smokestack finally cleared and the passengers began to disembark, one by one.

The visitors to Dodge City stepped onto the platform. After what he'd said all these years about not

THE RELUCTANT BRIDE
(Brides Along the Chisholm Trail)

being in the market for a family, Gabe stared at a curvy woman getting off the train from Kansas City with his friend, Logan. *What the heck was I thinking? And what is Logan doing back from his trip to clear Rose?*

The raids his southern unit took part in sickened him as much today as it did at the height of the War Between the States. A West Point cadet thrown into the war, Gabe had seen more senseless killing than he ever wanted to see again. After families like his were torn apart by either death or choosing opposite sides, he'd made a promise to himself to never put someone he loved into that situation.

Instead he took an oath, pinned on a star, and headed west to protect the citizens trying to recover after the devastation. And that oath kept Gabe from losing his heart to a woman and settling down with a family. That is, until he realized his role as marshal wasn't enough. He didn't want to spend the rest of his days alone. That he wanted a woman to come home to. So, he made the decision to resign from being a lawman, sent an advertisement for a bride, and aimed to live the rest of his days in peace.

And now hopefully she was standing on the depot platform. The woman standing next to Dodge City's very own Pinkerton Agent Logan Granger in animated conversation had to be his bride. The curvy woman in the neat dress, brown hair highlighted with a streak of silver pulled back into a bun under her hat, appeared to match the photograph he'd received a month ago. His heart raced like a stampede of longhorn. Only one way to find out if Miss Abigail Johnson had indeed arrived on time.

"If she's ours, Spade, I'd better go stake a claim on her before someone else does." He checked his vest for the ring and marriage license then patted the black gelding's neck and took a deep breath. "At least I know

Logan is spoken for."

His horse stomped a foot. Gabe's heart pounded. His hands were clammy. God help the people of Dodge if for any reason he had to draw his gun. The pearl-handled grip would surely slip right out of his hand. Then he'd either be lying up in Doc Elliott's, bleeding all over the place, or stretched out at the undertaker's. Neither option appealed to Gabe. And he was sure his new bride wouldn't appreciate it either.

"Logan!" Stetson pulled down low, Gabe spurred his horse and trotted up next to the train depot. Dismounting, he tipped his hat and smiled, immediately recognizing the woman from the photograph he'd received, "Ma'am."

"Marshal Gabe Hawkins meet—"

"Miss Abigail Johnson." Gabe smiled, stepping close enough to get a faint whiff of lavender. "I trust your trip was uneventful."

"Mr. Hawkins, it's nice to finally meet you." Abigail's voice was soft and full of nervous laughter. "It was quite the spectacle, seeing wild buffalo grazing out in the open and an Indian every now and again."

"You know each other?" Logan whistled, then chuckled. "Don't tell me you've—"

"We've been corresponding for several weeks." Gabe tore his gaze from Abigail, turning a scowl onto his friend. He wasn't ready to tell Logan the reasons he'd sent for a mail-order bride, and he suspected Abigail hadn't said anything as well.

Logan raised an eyebrow then waved some documents in the air. "I'm on my way over to the jail now to bring Rose some news regarding the trumped-up charges against her. As luck would have it, Miss Johnson was on her way to Dodge City to deliver the court documents in person. She recognized me in Topeka and has saved me a trip north. Miss Johnson,

THE RELUCTANT BRIDE
(Brides Along the Chisholm Trail)

will Rose and I see you later for dinner? You know she'll skin me alive if I don't insist."

Abigail smiled, nodding her head. "By all means, there is so much Rose and I have to catch up on since she left Wisconsin to marry you. Go give her the good news I brought from your superior and take her home. I'm sure the marshal will make sure I find my way to the hotel." She looked at Gabe for a moment then lowered her lashes.

The flirtatious gesture set his heart to pounding. Abigail's letters had shown her to be smart, witty, and a bit headstrong. His decision to take a wife seemed to be proving advantageous. "I'd be honored, Miss Johnson. I'll have your bags sent over to the Dodge House. In the meantime, how about a sundae at Etta May's after a long, dusty train ride?" Gabe pulled his hat from his head, then swept his hand through unruly curls to tame them back.

Her cheeks blushed a pretty rose petal pink, bringing a youthfulness to her wise brown eyes. "I've already taken care of my bags, but the sundae sounds heavenly. Do you mind giving me a chance to freshen up before sitting down for a good conversation?"

"Of course not. Take all the time you need. I agree we need a chance to talk and get to know each other a bit more, if that would be fine with you." Gabe reached out, placing a hand lightly on her lower back. She stood a good five to six inches shorter than his six-foot frame yet they seemed completely suited to each other as they strolled across the street over to the Dodge House, Spade trailing behind.

"Thank you, Mr. Hawkins. I won't be but a few minutes. I had already requested a room when I had my bags sent over." Abigail stepped from his touch and turned, smoothing down her skirt. "I'll be ready for that sundae and a bite to eat when I return, if that suits you.

I'm looking forward to our conversation." She turned that brilliant smile on him and sashayed through the doors of the hotel.

Now what was he going to do once he was left alone with his bride? Damn it! What could he possibly say to a woman who appeared as dignified as Miss Johnson? He knew from her letters that she'd worked as the head cook for the same large estate as Rose Granger. Miss Johnson's sophisticated manner took him by surprise.

Gabe Hawkins never had problems talking to the ladies before he'd sent for a wife. Why was this any different? Because it was just the two of them and Logan wasn't there to—to what? Guide a conversation between Gabe and Miss Johnson? Just because Miss Abigail Johnson was to become his wife didn't mean he couldn't talk to her normally. What kind of a life would they have if they couldn't communicate? A damn poor one, he figured. He wanted a wife he could talk to, laugh with, maybe even fall in love with over time.

Wife! Why the hell had he let the idea of retiring as a lawman possess him to send for a mail-order bride in the first place?

"So that's Gabe Hawkins," Abby mused with a song in her heart as she slipped out of the rumpled gray dress. "He is very pleasing to gaze upon. And he carries himself quite well with an air of quiet confidence becoming a lawman. Of course, he's not my Robert."

Sadness swept over Abby as she lay the dress across the only chair in the room. The thought of her late husband still panged deep in her heart even now. After all these years, the pain of his loss prickled deep in the recesses of her soul. The war was over; Robert hadn't come back. It would have put closure to the loss if she'd

THE RELUCTANT BRIDE
(Brides Along the Chisholm Trail)

been able to bury him in the Johnson family plot. Instead, he lay under the ground somewhere in Manassas along with so many other souls.

Robert Johnson had no business going off to fight in that damnable war. He'd had a wife at home and his elderly parents to look after. Instead he'd left that task to Abby, and when the time came to give them over to God, she'd been the one to handle their affairs, meager as they were. Robert had insisted a man of his education could be an asset to the war. He had reminded her that not every man who'd gone to take up arms could read and write. So he'd packed a satchel, saddled the old bay mare, and rode up to Camp Randall some thirty miles away. He trained as an officer then marched out to do his part. Remembering the painful past, Abby held back her tears. She'd not only lost Robert, but the family he'd promised they'd start as soon as he returned.

"Abigail Johnson! The dead are gone; best leave them buried after all these years." She swept away the threat of tears and inhaled deeply, resolving to do just that. It was past time for her to get on with her life, and Gabe Hawkins was the man to help her do so.

She laid out her maroon no-nonsense dress and began pulling the pins from her messy hair. Abby didn't like the weary look in her eyes, thinking it made her look older than her thirty-seven years. What must her soon-to-be husband think of his bedraggled mail-order bride? Gabe Hawkins looked so youthful with his sparkling blue eyes and dark unruly hair. He reminded Abby of a boy who'd just gotten away with something and could charm his way out of any sort of trouble. She smiled, thinking of the ways Gabe would probably use his charms on his new bride, thinking her none the wiser.

Abby slid into the warmth of the copper tub, her aching muscles relaxing. She smoothed the lavender soap she'd brought from home over her soot-embedded skin. Her mind gave way to the soothing scent and drifted off to a place of peace and youthful memories.

"Abigail Roberts, would you do me the honor of becoming my wife?"

Robert was on one knee, beads of moisture dotting his forehead. Abby stifled the urge to giggle at the man she'd loved for several months. The self-assured man of her heart anything but confident as he knelt before her. Did Robert really think she'd turn him away after all these months of courting?

"I believe that I will, provided Papa has given his blessing." Abby's heart sang so loud she was sure the entire town could hear the music. She and Robert Johnson were finally going to get married, have a home and eventually a family of their own.

"I wouldn't have dreamed of asking you otherwise. Your father gave his blessing last week when I called on him." Robert stood, wrapping his arms around her.

She would always be safe there. Robert would make sure of it.

And he had...until the day he announced his intentions regarding the War Between the States.

"I am going to join the cause, Abby. I must do what I can to help those who need it most. We take our privileged life here for granted. While we have plenty, others suffer at the cost of long days in a cotton field with hardly any food on their table. Their daily lives begin before sunrise and end far after sunset. They live in constant fear. If I can help to change at least one person's life then I've done my part."

Their sweet and loving life together abruptly ended when Robert marched away from their happy life into a war that swallowed him whole.

"You have mourned long enough, Abigail." Robert stood in his tattered blue uniform, a stain covering the place where his heart was. "Be happy, my love. Find

THE RELUCTANT BRIDE
(Brides Along the Chisholm Trail)

love again in this man; he'll take care of you." Then he blew her a kiss, turned and faded into the shadows.

"Miss Johnson?" A maid called out.

Her name, followed by a loud rap on the door, coaxed her out of her vision. The once warm water had turned cold and goose flesh trickled up her arms. Was she chilled from the cooled water or from Robert's visit? Since the end of the war Abby hadn't dreamed of her beloved deceased husband but a few times, each with an important message. The last dream had been when she'd sent Rose Duncan to Dodge City as a mail-order bride instead of going herself. Even in death, Robert was guiding her through dreams when it mattered most. This time was different. He'd never turned his back and walked away from her before.

"Yes, I'll be down in a few minutes," Abby called, climbing out of the tub.

Drying off, she hastily slipped into the dress she'd laid out then pinned a portion her hair back, allowing the fading dark waves to cascade over her shoulders. Glancing in the mirror, she smiled, feeling a bit like a schoolgirl. Robert had come to her in the dream. He'd told her to find love and to marry this man she'd been drawn to. It was what he wished for her...to find happiness and love in her heart once again. And so she would.

Abigail Johnson descended the steps to the lobby of Dodge House with the grace of a well-bred woman. Gabe's body flushed in unexpected need. For a woman a few years his senior, his bride was quite becoming. Her rich brown hair hung loose around her shoulders, accentuating her long, graceful neck. Deep coffee brown eyes reflected the schoolgirl lingering inside. She smiled and Gabe's heart exploded out of his chest and straight over to her.

"Miss Johnson, would you accompany me for a sundae?" Gabe offered his elbow, his nerves on fire at the thought this woman was soon to be his wife. All doubt of taking Abigail as his wife vanished from his mind. He'd never been surer he'd chosen the right woman. Would she feel the same when she learned once they were married he'd been transferred and would be taking her miles away to set her up in a house in Indian Territory?

"Mr. Hawkins." Abby placed her hand into the crux of his elbow, electricity jolting through him, "I do believe that would be the finest idea that has been presented to me since starting on my journey. However, you really must call me Abby if we are to be man and wife. Do you agree?"

Gabe nodded agreement as he guided her through the doors and onto the boardwalk. "Then you must call me Gabe."

"Gabe for Gabriel?" she asked keeping up with his long smooth stride.

"Yes. My parents named me Gabriel Samuel Hawkins after both of my grandfathers," Gabe said, remembering his grandfathers and the vastness of their plantations. Although both owned slaves, they abhorred the abusive practices by many of their peers and were disliked by many Southerners for their efforts in educating those in their care.

"It seems to fit you. Most lawmen can be perceived as heroes of God in the work they do to keep a town's people safe." Abby paused for moment, looking into Gabe's eyes. "I must confess, in my letters I didn't tell you that I wasn't born Abigail Johnson. Johnson is my late husband's family name. I was born Abigail Marie Roberts and have always been called Abby."

"You're a widow?" Gabe stumbled, raising his

eyebrows. *She isn't a pure woman? Does that mean— No! I will not allow my mind to take me where it doesn't belong—yet.*

"Robert went away to fight in the war. He lies with so many other lost souls at Manassas." Abby winced, her shoulders visibly drooping for a moment. "And what of you, Gabe? Did you fight in the war?"

"Yes, like many men did. I was in West Point when the war broke out." Gabe replayed that day when friends became enemies. When he was forced to choose which side he'd give his life for, right or wrong in the eyes of his family.

"Gabe!" Lilly Granger's little voice cried out running ahead of her parents. "Daddy said I could have ice cream with Momma's friend, Miss Johnson, after they get married today. He sent me over here to git you so's you can be his witness."

"Today?" Gabe cleared his throat, then rocked slightly back on his heels. He smiled wide, watching Lilly Granger scamper off with a skip and a jump. "Well, there really isn't any reason to wait now is there?"

Gabe guided Abby over to the Long Branch where a crowd was already gathering. It hadn't taken long for word of a wedding to reach the townsfolk. Together they gathered around Logan and Rose as Preacher Samuel began the ceremony. Gabe felt his vest for the folded piece of paper in the inside pocket. It wouldn't be long before he and Abby would be standing where Rose and Logan stood. They'd be saying their vows.

"I now pronounce you man and wife. Logan, you may kiss your bride." Preacher Samuel quietly closed his bible, and a swell of cheers soared up in the room when Logan swept Rose into his arms, claiming her with a kiss.

"Now it's our turn," Gabe whispered, taking

Abby's hand in his. "Preacher Samuels, if you have the time to marry another man and woman, would you?"

"No," Abby whispered, trying to pull her hand from his. Gabe had a grip on it and he wasn't about to let go.

He looked down at her, his heart filled with desire. "We agreed to an arrangement. The preacher is here. The town is here. We've got witnesses. Why wait?"

Preacher Samuel smiled, opening his bible back to the place he'd just read from. "I believe I do, Marshal. Anyone in particular?"

"Yes, sir." Gabe placed Abby's hand in the crux of his elbow and brought her to the spot where Rose had just become a married woman. "Miss Abigail Johnson and I are to be married, this very day."

For more information or to keep reading, visit my website:
http://maxinedouglasauthor.blogspot.com/p/2012-releases.html

ABOUT THE AUTHOR

Maxine Douglas first began writing in the early 1970s while in high school. She took every creative writing course that was offered at the time and focused her energy for many, many years on poetry. When a dear friend's sister revealed she was contracted to publish a romance it was all Maxine needed to get the ball rolling. She finished her first manuscript in a month's time.

A Wisconsin native, Maxine currently resides in Oklahoma with her husband. While Maxine and her husband may miss their family and friends in the north, they both love the mild winters Oklahoma has to offer. They have established a home in a town southeast of Oklahoma City. They have four grown children, two grand-daughters, two Quarter Horses (mother and son), and a German Shorthair Pointer. And many friends they now consider their OK family.

Maxine is a current member of Romance Writers of America, Oklahoma Romance Writers of America, having served as 2016 President and 2015 President-Elect, and the Oklahoma Writer's Federation, Inc.

Dear Reader,

I hope you enjoyed ***The Reluctant Bride***. I have to tell you, I really love the characters of Rose and Logan. Many readers wrote me asking: "What's next for them? What about Deputy Marshal Gabe Hawkins? Will he find a bride of his own? And Montana Sue, will she finally find the true love she so desperately seeks? And then there's Abigail Johnson, who gave up her chance for an 'adventure', will she finally find what she's looking for?" Well, stay tuned as my ***Brides Along the Chisholm Trail*** world continues. They'll all be back in ***The Marshal's Bride*** and ***The Cattleman's Bride***, both coming in 2017. Will there be happy endings? Wait and see.

When I was first asked to join the western historical boxset, ***Wanted: One Bride***, a surge of mixed emotions ran through me. I wanted to do it and was afraid I wouldn't to the genre justice. My wonderful boxset and Wednesday morning coffee mates, Callie Hutton and Heidi Vanlandingham, were always encouraging and never once said "then don't do it." I'm so thankful for them believing in me and giving my wings back to Dodge City in 1877.

After I wrote ***The Reluctant Bride***, I got so many letters from fans thanking me for the book. As an author, I love feedback. Frankly, you are the reason that I write. So, tell me what you liked, what you loved, even what you hated. I'd love to hear from you. You can write me at maxinedouglasauthor@gmail.com and visit me on the web at http://maxinedouglasauthor.blogspot.com.

Finally, I need to ask a favor, if you're so inclined, I'd love a review of ***The Reluctant Bride***. Loved it, hated it, whatever you really think—I'd just enjoy your feedback.

THE RELUCTANT BRIDE
(Brides Along the Chisholm Trail)

As you might know, reviews can be tough to come by these days. You, the reader, have the power now to make or break a book, or an author. If you have the time to do a review, you can add it to an author's page where you purchased this book as well as other online review outlets.

You can find all of my books listed on my blog http://maxinedouglasauthor.blogspot.com. Be sure to click on the newsletter tab when you visit.

If you are a member of Goodreads, please visit my author page: Maxine Douglas.

You will also find a listing of my books in the pages to follow.

If you visit any of my pages, please say "Hello," I'd love to hear from you!

Thank you so much for reading, and for spending time with me.

In gratitude,

Maxine

The Reluctant Bride
Wanted: One Bride, 3 book boxset (2017)

Roseanne "Rose" Duncan, witnesses her employer push his sickly wife down the staircase. Fearing she'll have to testify against a prominent man in town, she's given ad for a mail order bride in Dodge City. Believing this is a way for her to escape the possible danger of her employer, she travels to Dodge City and marries under the name of Abigail Johnson.

Logan Granger, is a Pinkerton Detective assigned to Dodge City area as an undercover bartender. When his mail order bride, "Abigail," steps off the train she doesn't fit the description of a matronly woman who has agreed to his marriage contract of no emotional attachments. There's no time to reconsider, the preacher is waiting to marry them.

Rose hadn't expected the handsome man waiting for her to be an undercover bartender with a six shooter on his hip and a badge on his lapel. Logan hadn't expected his soon to be wife to be young, beautiful, and a runaway murder witness.

THE RELUCTANT BRIDE
(Brides Along the Chisholm Trail)

The Marshal's Bride

After what he'd said about not being in the market for a mail order bride, Deputy Marshal Gabe Hawkins starred at the woman getting off the train from Kansas City. It has to be his bride who stood next to Logan Granger in animated conversation.

The neat dress, brown hair streaked with silver pulled back into a bun under her hat matched the tintype he'd received a month ago. His heart raced like a stampede of longhorn as Miss Abigail Johnson strolled to Etta May's.

Now what was he going to do?

The Cattleman's Bride (2017)

Cyrus Kennedy drove his herd into Dodge City, dirt and trail dust coating him from head to toe. He needed a bath, shave, and a good meal after he visited the Pinkerton agent assigned to his case.

Montana Sue grew feverish watching the cattle bawling and stomping their way through the middle of Dodge. It wasn't the longhorns making her insides on fire, it was the cowboy covered in dried mud and layers of dust sitting tall in the saddle.

Other Books by Maxine Douglas

Simply to Die For
Black Horse Canyon Series, Book 1
Romantic Suspense Romance

Leaving one life behind to begin anew, Kandi returns to her home town to open up a candy store. Unfortunately, circumstances pulls her back to the old ways, forcing her to track the trail of a serial porn star killer…

Jimmy, a reporter, discovers the woman he's fantasized about is on the "porn star" killer's hit list. Can he find the killer before the killer finds Kandi?

Nashville Rising Star
Contemporary

Utah Sheridan intends to win Nashville Rising Star at all costs; will his bribe be the end of Emerald Braun?

There were only three of them left now—Casey Montgomery from Oklahoma, the darling Emerald Braun, and Utah Sheridan. By this time next week, Utah was banking on only two left standing before the show even started. Emerald Braun wouldn't be one of them. He reached into his pocket and pulled out an envelope. Everything he'd wanted the past few years depends on what's inside it.

Nashville by Morning
Contemporary

Heather Jones is a frustrated writer who falls in love with the southern ways and decides to stay, intending to break into the country music business.

James Sheridan is the son of a legendary performer striving to make it on his own. After a breakout song is recorded a Montana storm causes an accident and James leaves the tour bus, and his band, in search of help. Instead he encounters the harsh storm and becomes lost.

In a deep depression, Heather retreats to Wisconsin, where she spends months dealing with the probability that her husband will never be found.

Will Heather find the peace to move on with her life?

Will James return to find the woman whose memory kept him hopeful of the future and reach Nashville by Morning?

THE RELUCTANT BRIDE
(Brides Along the Chisholm Trail)

Knight to Remember
Time Travel Romance

In 15th Century England, The Black Knight a/k/a Sir Reynold, has fallen from grace with his childhood friend, Queen Isabel, and is in a no-win situation. He must compete against his friend, and blood brother Thomas. If he wins, Sir Reynold will be banished from Heartsease; if he loses, Thomas will be stripped of his knighthood...

Courtney Parker is a 21st Century seamstress at the Bristol Renaissance Faire. Unlike other reenactors, she performs her profession year-round, making costumes for others. She's always loved the story of the mysterious Black Knight of Heartsease and has looked forward to it every year. But this year's different...

Issie Cummings, the Ren Faire's potion shopkeeper, will stop at nothing to gain what escaped her centuries ago...Sir Reynold Loddington's love and body.

Will Reynold be able to turn back the hands of time and right what went wrong—or will he find himself banned from another country and the woman he loves?

Blood Ties
U.S. Historical Time Travel

A long-lost aunt, two loving ghosts, two people looking for answers, the Civil War and a family legacy all with BLOOD TIES

Emma Sorenson's search for a long lost aunt leads her to the ancestral home of Royal Kinsman and a path to Civil War.

A story portraying a love so strong that it carries through the Kinsman family from the mid-1860s through generations leading to modern times. Emma travels through three early battles of the American Civil War up to one of the bloodiest days in American history when Royal rescues her at Antietam.

Rings of Paradise
Contemporary Romance

Dear Reader,

I'm not much on putting words to paper, action is more up my alley. I'm Flame, the reigning champion in the Universal Wrestling World (UWW). So why am I here?

I grew up in a wrestling family and cut my teeth on the squared circle, which by the way is the only "lady" I trust any more.

I've gone and bought out a small press magazine in Madison, Wisconsin that was going nowhere fast, hired a woman by the name of Khristen Roberts, who according to the editor-in-chief is untrained and wants nothing more than to be a journalist.

Okay, I'm a sucker in helping people out, it's my one weakness, if I have any. Problem is she's on vacation in Hawaii. I've got to catch up with her somewhere along the line for her to join up with me and the UWW. I just hope Khristen is up for the ride…it's always a trip.

Yours truly,

The Flame

The Queen
Seasons of Passion Series Paranormal Romance

Cole Masterson takes a ghost hunting gig aboard the Queen Mary to find out why pictures of his great-grandfather and Hanna Amery are in an old locket.

Hanna Amery finds the love she left behind on The Grey Ghost housed in the body of Cole Masterson, she just needs to figure out how to get to him.

What happens when they find each other on opposite planes of the Universe?

Road Angel
Seasons of Passion Series, Paranormal Romance

Truck driver Lee Thomas believes his life is over after the ghost of his wife who died three years ago steps in front of him and jack-knives his truck on a snowy Wisconsin road on his way home.

Cyn Bedford, an angel, must convince him to fight for his life. She's broken an angel rule and has fallen in love with her charge.

Will Cyn truly be Lee's Road Angel for life?

Eternally Yours
Paranormal Erotica

Cassandra Jameson and her best friend, Paige Matteson, have opened a store in an ancient part of town called Eternal Pleasures. Cassandra is obsessed with pleasuring herself as no man has ever been able to accomplish, and finds herself an old, tattered book of erotic Victorian tales. She becomes obsessed with a male character which appears in each of the stories she reads and begins to fantasize about him.

Garrett Alexander lived his life performing the teachings of pleasures of the body hundreds of years before. His shop Eternal Pleasures was located in the very same spot that the new Eternal Pleasures has now opened. Having heard the siren call of CJ, Garrett finds he cannot resist the burning desire to pleasure her as no mortal man has ever done before.

Paige Matteson has some promises to fulfill to her best friend…and herself. The mysterious Russell Canterbury may just be the one to take her into a world of sex she'd thought impossible. But Russell has other ideas. He's travelled hundreds of years to seek revenge of CJ for the death of his dear friend, Garrett. Or is it jealousy that spurs him now that Garrett has found peace instead of walking in the shadows of the undead for centuries? What sacrifices are they willing to make for love?

Writing as Debi Wilder

Gabby's Second Chance
Paranormal Erotica

Believing she doesn't deserve to love again, Gabby Adams gets a second chance to find happiness with only one wish. (adult content)

By the Blue Moon
Blue Moon Magic Series, Book 1 Werewolf Erotica

Chastity Langford's thirst for sex is more than just a fascination; it's a coming of age for the wolfen princess. Only she doesn't know why all of a sudden she wants to take the man she loves to hate and roll around on the ground with him. She doesn't understand that this unquenchable thirst is primal and primitive…but she's about to.

Justin Sinclair has waited his entire life for the red-haired girl to grow up. Now that he's been summoned to the United States by Charles Langford to take his rightful place as clan leader, he's looking forward to teaching his betrothed what it means to a wolfen princess.

The coming of the blue moon brings with it dangers

to the Alpha clan. Dangers that only Justin and his army can destroy before the Langford princesses are taken prisoner and bred by the Beta leader who destroyed his family.

As Justin battles with his demons on the ground, Chastity wars with her own changes. Having Justin overseeing her moves in her father's company is that last thing she wanted. Bedding him on her terms is one thing, having to work with him is something she didn't bargain for…not even By the Blue Moon.

Made in the USA
San Bernardino, CA
21 June 2017